IMAGES
of America

BEVERLY SHORES

A SUBURBAN DUNES RESORT

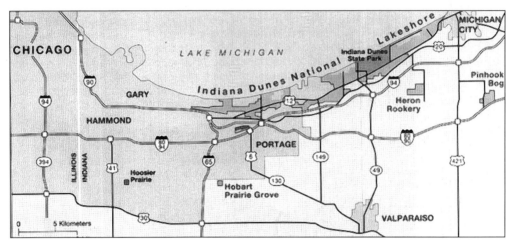

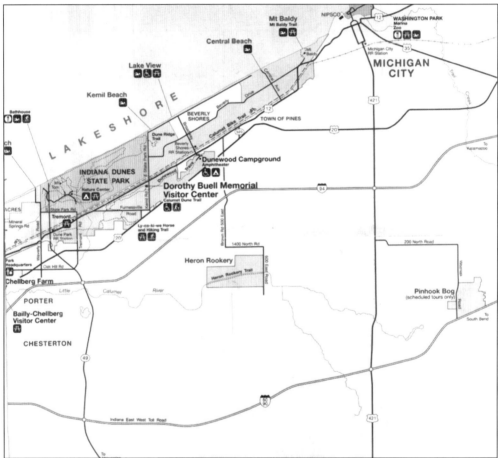

(Maps courtesy of the Indiana Dunes National Lakeshore)

IMAGES
of America

BEVERLY SHORES

A SUBURBAN DUNES RESORT

Jim Morrow

ARCADIA

Published by Arcadia Publishing,
an imprint of Tempus Publishing, Inc.
3047 N. Lincoln Ave., Suite 410
Chicago, IL 60657

Printed in Great Britain.

Library of Congress Catalog Card Number: 2001088168

For all general information contact Arcadia Publishing at:
Telephone 843-853-2070
Fax 843-853-0044
E-Mail sales@arcadiapublishing.com

For customer service and orders:
Toll-Free 1-888-313-2665

Visit us on the internet at http://www.arcadiapublishing.com

CONTENTS

ACKNOWLEDGMENTS

The following individuals have contributed their knowledge, photographs, and enthusiasm about Beverly Shores, its environment, and significant history.

Steven G. McShane
Archivist/Curator of the Calumet Regional Archives of Indiana University Northwest, Gary, Indiana

Jane Walsh-Brown
Assistant Director of the Westchester Public Library and Curator of the Westchester Township Historical Museum, Chesterton, Indiana

Carol Ruzic and Carl Reed of Beverly Shores

Wendy Weis-Smith
Indiana Dunes State Park

Judy Collins and Janice Slupski
Indiana Dunes National Lakeshore

Tom Anderson and Charlotte Read
Save-the-Dunes Council

In memory of Leo Post—builder of many of the architecturally historic and significant Mediterranean Revival-styled homes, and commercial and public buildings in Beverly Shores— and his daughter Ann Carlson.

INTRODUCTION

Beverly Shores, Indiana, is a small resort community clustered along the southernmost tip of Lake Michigan, approximately 40-miles southeast of Chicago. The town is now an island of private resort homes surrounded by the Indiana Dunes National Lakeshore, a federal park. This community of surprising Mediterranean Revival villas and more traditional houses nestled into wooded dunes was planned in a suburban manner, with the picturesque lanes winding through the sand hills, easily accessible along broad, direct access roads. However, the disjointed transition from the thoroughly-developed dunes to the pristine flat lands and woods behind them, as well as the isolation of the community's administrative buildings, indicates that this planned resort was never completed. Today Beverly Shores presents a fascinating collection of tangible artifacts reflecting the changes in American (more specifically Chicago) society between the late 1920s and World War II. This book is an exploration of this physical evidence of how the period's planning and architectural values shaped Beverly Shores.

Beverly Shores was planned as a retreat from the congestion of Chicago. It was to have functioned as both a resort and a railroad suburb since its residents could reach downtown Chicago in an hour via the interurban railroad.

The first true railroad suburb, Riverside, Illinois, was created outside Chicago in 1868 by Frederick Law Olmstead. In Riverside the railroad station and commercial center became the "front door" of the suburb, and as such were carefully designed to create a distinctive image for the new town. Developers realized that by strictly controlling the physical (and often social) characteristics of their new towns, that they could create harmonious, predictable environments highly attractive to the growing number of "white-collar" urbanites. These suburbs were places where people of similar social status could raise a family safely sheltered from the unpleasant traits of the city, yet continue to take advantage of its business opportunities. Many of these suburban development characteristics would have a major impact on later resorts such as Beverly Shores.

The 1920s was the decade in which American resort communities boomed. Americans were flush with their newfound international power and wealth. Improved transportation made formerly remote spots accessible in a matter of hours, and the rigid Victorian behavioral codes were breaking apart. The State of Florida quickly catapulted from a rather sleepy backwater to the playground of choice for most of the country. The 24-hour train trip from the Northeast, and its tax system, were features which combined with its balmy climate to draw upper and middle class vacationers en masse. New vacation towns such as Coral Gables, Boca Raton, and Palm Beach shaped the popular image of how a resort should appear, and developers all over the country borrowed from this image to lend glamour to their own projects. Beverly Shores is a clear example of such emulation.

In 1919, a rather obscure architect named Addison Mizner was hired to design several buildings for the new resort of Palm Beach, Florida. Even though most of the resort's clientele would be from the Northeast, Mizner felt that traditional northern styles were inappropriate for the tropical climate. Instead, he drew on the traditional architectural forms of the Mediterranean coast and Spain for inspiration. This style was a logical choice since the two areas boast such similar climates, and since the many wealthy vacationers who were accustomed to resorting on the Riviera instead began frequenting Florida due to the upheaval of the First World War. Mizner's Everglades Club pioneered his version of Mediterranean Revival architecture with its use of Baroque motifs, textured stucco, rustic beams, barrel roof tile, and open plans which flowed out onto patios and arcades.

Developers copied Mizner's style throughout Florida in the 1920s. In 1921, John Merrick set out to create Coral Gables, the most architecturally ambitious of the new resorts. Mediterranean motifs were again utilized in the erection of major public landmarks such as entry gates, which were built to give distinction to a site which was topographically unexciting. This town did not limit itself to Spanish architecture but created exotic theme sections such as Dutch, Chinese, Colonial, French Provincial, and American Colonial, possibly establishing a precedent for the Colonial Village homes at Beverly Shores. Merrick promoted his town by sending out three-thousand salesmen to the Northeast who offered free train trips to those who would inspect and hopefully purchase his lots. In order to spur development he also built community centers and resort facilities such as indoor sports complexes and luxurious hotels, and set aside land for a school. Unfortunately, most of the Florida resorts were devastated by an economic collapse in 1927, which stopped the completion of their development along their original plans. However, the development and promotional innovations of this great resort boom were copied by other resort developers such as Frederick Bartlett of Beverly Shores.

This contemporary fascination with Mediterranean Revival resort architecture among both the general and architectural public makes it perfectly logical that Frederick Bartlett chose to create a village of "Seaside Spanish" villas at Beverly Shores. Even though the original motivation for importing Spanish forms was because of the similarity of climate and use of Florida resorts to the Mediterranean, it became perfectly acceptable for the wooded dunes along the shore of Lake Michigan to shelter a community of buildings which had no historical relationship to their sites. The dictating factor was that Mediterranean Revival architecture symbolized "resort."

One

DISCOVERING THE INDIANA DUNES

DOIN' THE DUNES-PRAIRIE CLUB

WIND-FORMED DUNES. "The Dunes Country of Indiana represents the work of 100 times 1,000 years, by such artists as the glaciers, water, wind, and sun, until you find there a park perfect, beautiful; a fairy land; a land of dreams; a land of remoteness; a land of solitude; a land of long beaches; a land on whose frail shore strong waves beat at times with a thunderous roar; a land so fair and fine no city park could be made to equal it by the expenditure of countless millions." Most of the photographs in this chapter were taken prior to World War I by the renowned Dunes photographer Arthur E. Anderson of Tremont, Indiana. He lived in Tremont for 40 years, coming from the Hyde Park area of Chicago. Art had joined the Prairie Club in 1913 where he met his future wife, Ruth Babcock, a Chicago teacher. (Photo courtesy of Calumet Regional Archives of Indiana University Northwest, Gary, Indiana.)

ANDERSON'S SPECTACULAR DUNES VIEWS. Art Anderson and Ruth were married in the Dunes— an outdoor, sunrise ceremony on a Sunday morning in 1922, conducted by a minister who had come out from Chicago. Art had designed their gold wedding rings himself, engraving them with Dunes motifs. In 1913, Art organized within the Prairie Club, a Camera Club, and later, a Canoe Club. (Photos courtesy of Calumet Regional Archives of Indiana University Northwest, Gary, Indiana.)

EARLY CAR CAMPERS IN THE DUNES. Art Anderson was one of the first campers in the Dunes. He used his Model-T Ford as their camper and tied a canvas to the car, and two sticks held up his shelter. Art was known to have stayed away as long as 10 days at a time with Ruth, taking pictures of bear, deer, elk, flowers, buds, and other flora. (Photo courtesy of Calumet Regional Archives of Indiana University Northwest, Gary, Indiana.)

DUNES MEETS LAKE. This dune and lake view was taken by Art Anderson on November 8, 1914. A lover of the dunes and a strong conservationist, his pictures of the Dunes which he took with him to an appearance before the Indiana State Legislature were influential in the creation of the Indiana Dunes State Park. He was in many photo shows and won many awards. He was active in the Prairie Club's historical committee and helped in doing the book the Club published in 1941, *Outdoors with the Prairie Club*, which was illustrated with his pictures. (Photo courtesy of Calumet Regional Archives of Indiana University Northwest, Gary, Indiana.)

WIND-WHIPPED DUNE TREES. After the Revolutionary War, the terms of a treaty with Great Britain ceded land around the Great Lakes to the United States. In 1783, the Potawatomi tribe dominated the area at the foot of Lake Michigan. By the famous Ordinance of 1783, sometimes called "The Magna Charta of the West," the region north of the Ohio River became a political unit, later to divide itself into the sister states of Ohio, Indiana, Illinois, Michigan, Wisconsin, and Minnesota. (Photo courtesy of Calumet Regional Archives of Indiana University Northwest, Gary, Indiana.)

13

SAND DUNE "BLOWOUT." By 1800, the population of the Northwest Territory had so increased that Sir William St. Clair could no longer preserve order, and just at the time that Spain was ceding Louisiana back to France, it was divided and all west of the present state of Ohio was rechristened the Territory of Indiana, with William Henry Harrison for its governor. This territory extended west to the Mississippi and north to Canada, an unbroken wilderness save for old French settlements such as Cahokia, Kaskaskia, and Vincennes—microscopic as compared to the vast region.

The military journal kept by Lieutenant Swearingen in 1803 relates that troops from Detroit under his command camped successively at "Kinzie's Improvement" (New Buffalo, Michigan) and at the mouth of the Portage Rivers, where Michigan City is now. On August 15, he proceeded 39 miles and encamped near an old fort. The next day they camped on the "Little Calamas" (Little Calumet River), having crossed the "Grand Calamas" (Grand Calumet River). Near this crossing now stands the Bailly Homestead, built about 20 years later. (Photo courtesy of Calumet Regional Archives of Indiana University Northwest, Gary, Indiana.)

Wind-Shaped Dune, "Lookout." The first movement on the part of the United States to protect the new frontier was the building, by order of President Thomas Jefferson in 1803, of Fort Dearborn at the mouth of the Chicago River, the outmost post of civilization. The establishment of the Government Post at Chicago had considerable influence upon the settlement of Porter and adjoining counties in Indiana, through which the thoroughfare led that was to be the main artery by which emigration flowed to "the far west," as the Mississippi was then called. The thoroughfare that connected the east and west was the Detroit-Chicago Road, coincident with the Great Sauk Trail and its branches. (Photo courtesy of Calumet Regional Archives of Indiana University Northwest, Gary, Indiana.)

MARCH OF THE DUNES. In 1806, it was learned that a plot had been devised to surprise Detroit, Mackinaw, Fort Wayne, and Chicago. This plot culminated in 1812, with the fall of Fort Dearborn, notwithstanding the heroic efforts of its sister post, Fort Wayne, to lend succor. The two posts were in constant relation, transfer of officers and men being frequent, and the Dunes afforded sanctuary to Dearborn refugees. (Photos courtesy of the Westchester Public Library, Chesterton, Indiana.)

DUNE OWL AND DRIFTWOOD. In 1822, while Illinois was still part of Indiana, Joseph Bailly removed his fur trading station from Parc aux Vaches to the region of the Calumet River as Baillytown, and there built a log house that for more than a century has been a landmark on the Sauk Trail of Chicago Road. Of City West, that fabled metropolis of the lakes, which Daniel Webster visited in 1837 (Waverly, Furnessville, etc.), we believe that the historical survey of this region has shown that the Story of the West—Progress of the Frontier—could not be written without the dunes of Porter County. (Photos courtesy of Calumet Regional Archives of Indiana University Northwest, Gary, Indiana.)

HIKERS AND WALKERS. In 1908, members of 15 Chicago-area organizations banded together to organize a series of walks and hikes to explore nature. Participants in these "Saturday Afternoon Walking Trips" all recognized the interdependence of people and their environment, and they understood the importance of outdoor recreation. In 1909, the group made its first ascent of Mt. Tom, the tallest of the Indiana Dunes. By 1911, the hiking club incorporated under the name of "Prairie Club." Founding member and famous landscape artist, Jens Jensen, suggested the club name. (Photos courtesy of Calumet Regional Archives of Indiana University Northwest, Gary, Indiana.)

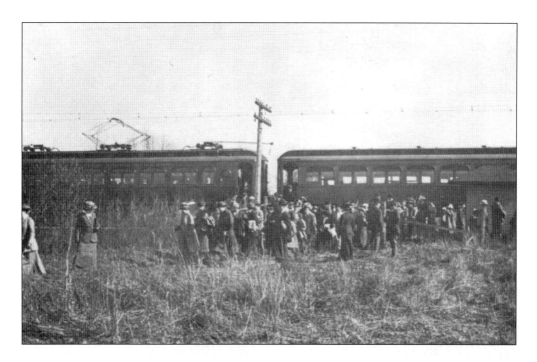

SOUTH SHORE LINE. Prairie Club members often came to the dunes via the South Shore train. In 1910, so many hikers joined the July 4th walk in the dunes that a special train was dispatched from Chicago to the Tremont station.

At this time the railway was owned and operated by the Chicago, Lake Shore and South Bend Line using wooden passenger cars. After Samuel Insull acquired the line in 1925 and changed the name to Chicago, South Shore and South Bend Line, he replaced the wooden cars with steel cars. (Photos courtesy of the Westchester Public Library, Chesterton, Indiana.)

19

PRAIRIE CLUB BEACH HOUSE. In 1912, the Prairie Club established its first overnight camp (Link House) in the Dunes when it turned an abandoned boathouse on the beach into a small shelter and bath house. This first "unofficial" beach house would be in the forthcoming Indiana State Park. The following year a Prairie Club Conservation Committee was formed and a more substantial beach house was constructed in 1913, also in what is now the Indiana Dunes State Park. October dedication of the Beach House featured the first performance of the pageant of "The Spirit of the Dunes." Gradually, club members built more than 100 summer cottages on the beach, near the shelter. This new "home" site was located on a dune ridge high above Lake Michigan on land leased for $25 per acre. Eventually the Prairie Club purchased 49 acres of beach and dunes in what today is part of the Indiana Dunes State Park. (Photos courtesy of Calumet Regional Archives of Indiana University Northwest, Gary, Indiana.)

NEW PRAIRIE CLUB HOUSE. The New Prairie Club Beach House, as it appeared in 1913, located near Tremont on the beach of Lake Michigan. Stairways lead to this secluded wooded location.

Happy hikers climb Mt. Tom in 1915. This high dune crowned the Indiana Dunes State Park 10 years later. Characteristic of the hikers at that time was the formal attire worn for recreational use. (Photos courtesy of Calumet Regional Archives of Indiana University Northwest, Gary, Indiana.)

BATHING BEAUTY. "It is felt that there are probably many persons who . . . have not ventured forth to enjoy the beauties of nature that lie profusely scattered at the very gates of the city, and that a series of walks, led by guides who are familiar with the regions visited . . . will at least serve the purpose of an introduction to Chicago's really beautiful environment."

By 1914, conservation had become a primary focus of the Prairie Club activities. The club fought for more than a decade to preserve the Indiana Dunes. Their lobbying recruited scientists and artists of great repute. Their promotional pageant of 1917 drew over five-thousand spectators and was unsurpassed in effectiveness. Prairie Club member Jens Jensen, along with other members, took Colonel Richard Lieber (the Director of Indiana Department of Conservation) on a walk through the Indiana Dunes. Lieber soon became one of the biggest advocates of dune preservation and in 1923 legislation was signed to create the Indiana Dunes State Park. (Photo courtesy of Calumet Regional Archives of Indiana University Northwest, Gary, Indiana.)

DUNES POSTERETTES. More than a 100,000 Dunes Posterettes were distributed. Every posterette bears the slogan "Save the Dunes for a National Park." Thousands of citizens received this message for the first time in 1917. First impressions are lasting; and coming to them in the pleasantly attractive form of our little Dunes scenes were going to create a predisposition in favor of the project.

The Dunes Posterettes afforded one sure method of individual effort. It was a small matter to request that every piece of your mail bear with it the message of the Dunes. The waves and the wind and the sand were building the Dunes. The mail and the posterettes and the will to serve, irresistibly moved to convert them into a national park.

Posterettes were on sale at the Prairie Club office, the office of the treasurer, or by any member of the committee. (Photos courtesy of Indiana Dunes State Park.)

PRAIRIE CLUB PUBLICATIONS. The Prairie Club annual report disclosed its past activities, membership, and financial condition. The Bulletins published by the Prairie Club list scheduled trips to the dunes for hikes, picnics, and other recreational activities. As printed on the cover of each Bulletin, the Prairie Club was organized for the promotions of outdoor recreation in the form of walks and outings, the dissemination of knowledge of the attractions of the country adjacent to the City of Chicago, and the preservation of suitable areas in which such recreation may be pursued. (Courtesy of the Westchester Public Library, Chesterton, Indiana.)

Inscription on plaque:

STEPHEN TYNG MATHER
JULY. 4. 1867   JAN. 22. 1930

HE LAID THE FOUNDATION OF THE NATIONAL PARK SERVICE. DEFINING AND ESTABLISHING THE POLICIES UNDER WHICH ITS AREAS SHALL BE DEVELOPED AND CONSERVED UNIMPAIRED FOR FUTURE GENERATIONS. THERE WILL NEVER COME AN END TO THE GOOD THAT HE HAS DONE.

STEPHEN T. MATHER. Public hearings were held in Chicago in 1916 by the National Parks Bureau of the Department of the Interior, presided over by Stephen Mather, a Hyde Park resident, to discuss establishment of a national park in the Indiana Dunes. "Articles written and speeches made by members of the Prairie Club were a great help in support of this project." Mather was in the Prairie Club Conservation Committee while being the assistant to the Secretary of the Interior. A self-made millionaire in the borax business, Mather promoted a separate national park system, which Congress approved in 1916. As a result, he became the first director of the National Park Service.

Excerpts from the report to Congress by Stephen T. Mather, Assistant to the Secretary of the Interior. "These sand dunes are classified as among the finest in the world. They are deposits which constitute the action of the elements for ages past and are beautiful at all times of the year. The beauty of the trees and other plant life in their autumn garb, as I saw them recently, was beyond description. The constitute a Paradise for the artist and writer. The sand dunes are admittedly wonderful. Of surpassing interest to the visitor are the dunes which are in the building or are being destroyed by the winds. A stretch of unoccupied beach 25 miles in length, a broad clean safe beach, affords splendid bathing facilities. There are hundreds of good camp sites on the beach and back in the dunes. In my judgment, a large section of this dune region should be preserved for all time. Science and education virtually demand that it be safeguarded forever. The dunes are accessible to 5,000,000 people and are ideally located in the center of population." (Photo courtesy of the Westchester Public Library, Chesterton, Indiana.)

JENS JENSEN. Jens Jensen, landscape architect, one-time superintendent of the Chicago Park District, and the first champion of the Dunes preservation, helped organize the Prairie Club. In 1911, the Prairie Club charter, "Established the maintenance of temporary and permanent camps, promotion of outdoor recreation, encouragement of the nature, preservation of suitable areas in which recreation can be preserved." The Dunes became the center of the Club's recreation and conservation focus, influenced by Jensen. He became the fourth president of the Prairie Club in 1914. View of Jens Jensen at the dedication of the Dunes Memorial Fountain which he designed, at the Dunes State Park, May 30, 1932. (Photo courtesy of the Westchester Public Library, Chesterton, Indiana.)

CAMPERS PITCH MAKESHIFT TENTS ON FORE DUNE. The Prairie Club has given each year since their Beach House was opened in the Dunes, an annual open-air festival, with attendance ranging from a few hundred to 1,500 in the spring of 1916.

From such experience the Club believed that with proper local publicity many more thousands would attend the more elaborate production planned for 1917, thus being brought into contact with the romantic beauty of this historic region for the first time, and thereby, with national publicity, giving great help to the movement to "Save the Dunes" as a public park for all to enjoy. This belief having gained currency among many nature-loving groups, The Dunes Pageant Association was the result. (Photo courtesy of Calumet Regional Archives of Indiana University Northwest, Gary, Indiana.)

MARSH FLOWERS (Photo courtesy of Calumet Regional Archives of Indiana University Northwest, Gary, Indiana.)

BOOK of
The HISTORICAL PAGEANT
of The DUNES
PORT CHESTER INDIANA
on LAKE MICHIGAN·
MAY 30 and
JUNE 3, 1917.

TWENTY FIVE CENTS

Here shall the prophet's vision flame, the song
Of free and lofty trails, and purple smokes
Of dreaming fires ascend. The Dreamers come:
Show them through me the years of this thy home
Great Manitou: the tribes who trod this trail.

PRAIRIE CLUB PAGEANT. In 1917, the Prairie Club initiated the Dunes Pageant Association for the purpose of staging a large, outdoor, historical pageant of the Indiana Dunes, *The Dunes Under Four Flags.* Over 10,000 persons attended the two performances of the pageant, which received wide coverage in the press and did much to publicize the beauty and importance of the Dunes. (Courtesy of the Westchester Public Library, Chesterton, Indiana.)

AUDIENCE FOR PAGEANT. Audiences gather for the pageant at the dunes, May 30, 1917. This occurred near Port Chester, which was a South Shore Line train stop just west of the Tremont station. As of the year 1917, the pageant, *The Dunes Under Four Flags*, commemorates the Spanish, French, British, and finally the American rule over this area. (Photos courtesy of Calumet Regional Archives of Indiana University Northwest, Gary, Indiana.)

DUNES UNDER FOUR FLAGS PAGEANT. Although Indiana became a state in 1816, this land legally remained Indian territory until the expulsion of the Potawatomi tribe in 1838. Soon after, a Michigan City banker and businessman name Chauncy Blair purchased the large tract of land, which stretched westward from Michigan City to Tremont, from the Federal Government. This land's physical characteristics made it particularly difficult to develop for agricultural or commercial use in the 1800s, and it remained largely as a wilderness disturbed only by land traffic passing through on its way to Chicago. Michigan City served as the termination of westward roads leading to Chicago from southern Indiana and Lake Erie, from which these roads combined into a difficult path through the dunelands. At first this path ran on the open sandy beach, but the unpredictability of the shoreline and the softness of the sand soon motivated the construction of an inland road. This first road ran behind the dunes, and was thus subject to flooding and deep mud in this marshy area. In spite of its use as a transport route, the natural difficulties of the duneland area precluded significant early development beyond the scattered huts of trappers and a few isolated farms. (Courtesy of the Westchester Public Library, Chesterton, Indiana.)

SCENES FROM PAGEANT. Strong arguments for the establishment of a national park in the sand dunes of northern Indiana, between Millers and Michigan City, is contained in a report made to Congress by Secretary of the Interior Lane, the report being prepared by Stephen T. Mather, director of National Parks. Mr. Mather gives unbounded praise to the sand dunes as objects of scenic beauty and scientific interest, and estimates that from 9,000 to 13,000 acres of the sand dune country should be included in the project. The cost of the purchase of a strip a mile wide and 15 to 20-miles long on the southern shore will be from $1.5 million to $2 million. The estimated cost of maintenance of the park is $15,000 a year. (Courtesy of the Westchester Public Library, Chesterton, Indiana.)

PAGEANT PARTICIPANT. White Smoke and her father, Thunder-Water, took part in the pageant of 1917.

For many years there has been an active propaganda for the conservation of natural beauty about Chicago, the preservation of the Indiana Sand Dunes as a protected state or national park being especially desired.

This pageant association believed that in no better way could the value and beauty of the Dunes be shown the residents of Indiana and Illinois than by an historical pageant which would in the first part accent the remarkable connection of the Dunes country with American history, and in the second part project the wonder and beauty of the Dunes, through poetry, music, and dancing. (Photo courtesy of Calumet Regional Archives of Indiana University Northwest, Gary, Indiana.)

FRANK DUDLEY. Frank Dudley, the renowned artist of dunes landscapes, poses at the George Mather Memorial at the Dunes State Park, 1932. The Prairie Club members were instrumental in forming the Indiana Dunes National Park Association in 1916. Tom Taggart, boss of the Indiana Democratic Party, introduced, as a U.S. Senator, the first federal Dune legislation in 1916. However, when the U.S. entered World War I, the momentum for a national park was lost. In 1922, the Prairie Club purchased 46 acres of land on which the Tremont Beach House stood, at a cost of $600 per acre. Finally in 1923, the Indiana legislature passed a bill to create the Indiana Dunes State Park. (Photo courtesy of Calumet Regional Archives of Indiana University Northwest, Gary, Indiana.)

PRAIRIE CLUB MARSHALL FIELD STORE EXHIBIT. Henry Cowles, a resident of Hyde Park, as well as Stephen Mather, was a pioneer in the field of plant ecology and for 40 years was a champion for the preservation of Indiana Dunes. Richard Lieber brought the Department of Conservation to Indiana and paved the way for the establishment of an Indiana Dunes State Park. He became its first director. In 1926, the Prairie Club support for a state park in the dunes culminated in the Club's sale of its property to the State of Indiana, with a seven year's tenure. In 1932, the Prairie Club Tremont tenure ended and was commemorated by the dedication of the Memorial Drinking Fountain on Memorial Day.

All of the efforts of the Prairie Club in the promotion of the preservation of the dunes were to help form a national park, which was ultimately accomplished in the 1960s. However, their effort did result in the creation of the Indiana Dunes State Park in 1923. The Club's activities helped the South Shore Line gain passengers to visit the dunes, which in turn became a major marketing program for the South Shore Line. Even later, all of the interest and desirability of the dunes attracted the development of Beverly Shores by the Bartlett brothers in 1929. (Photo courtesy of Calumet Regional Archives of Indiana University Northwest, Gary, Indiana.)

Two

MARKETING THE
INDIANA DUNES

SAMUEL INSULL—SOUTH SHORE LINE

SOUTH SHORE TRAIN AT TREMONT STATION. No recreational attraction along the South Shore Line was more popular than the celebrated Indiana Dunes area at the south end of Lake Michigan, and none was more extensively promoted by the railway. Posters, a Duneland folder, maps of hiking trails, and frequent newspaper advertising were all employed to promote interest in the Dunes, and the South Shore Line played an important role in the establishment of the Indiana Dunes State Park. (Photo courtesy of M.D. McCarter.)

What They Are	Things to See and Do	How to Go

WHAT are the Dunes of Indiana? You have heard them talked about. But have you ever been in this "land of the whispering sands"? Some people have an idea that the Dunes country is nothing more than a vast sea of sand. Nothing could be farther from correct.

There are sand hills, yes—huge, weird, fascinating mountains of golden sand. But while on one side of you there is a veritable desert, on the other there is a luxurious forest of trees, ferns and flowers!

"A little bit of *everywhere* brought together here at the southernmost end of Lake Michigan"—that, in a few words, describes the alluring Dunes country.

Would you love to visit the towering pines of the Canadian woods?

The famous Berkshire Hills of Massachusetts?

The cactus country of New Mexico and Arizona?

The valley of a quiet stream in Norway?

The tamarack lands of our northern states?

The broad, sandy beaches of Florida and Southern California?

The wilderness of the forest primeval?

The home of the trailing arbutus in old New England?

The great African desert of the Sahara?

The dune country of far-off Algeria?

The Lonesome Pine

You need not travel thousands upon thousands of miles to visit these wonders and beauties of nature. You need not take weeks and months of time. For they are here, at home, almost at your door, in the Dunes country of Indiana!

Nature has been most generous with us in the Middle West. She has given us a wonderland of which there is no duplicate. Have you taken advantage of what she has provided? Don't miss this opportunity for a treat you will long remember!

There are excellent reasons why people talk about the Dunes—why they come back again and again after their first visit. There is only one way to learn these reasons. That is to *visit the Dunes yourself.*

More than 300 varieties of birds frequent the Dunes country. Wild flowers and trees grow there in great abundance—species that are found nowhere else in this region.

The State of Indiana has set apart a 2,000-acre tract of Duneland as a State Park. A map of it appears on the inside pages of this folder. You are welcome to this park at all seasons of the year. Ten cents is the only admission, and this small sum helps to maintain the park. The park entrance is at Tremont, "Gateway to the Dunes."

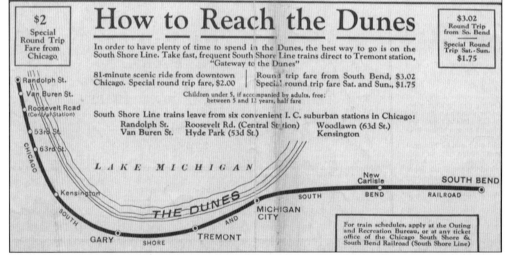

How to Reach the Dunes

$2 Special Round Trip Fare from Chicago		$3.02 Round Trip from So. Bend — Special Round Trip Sat.-Sun. $1.75

In order to have plenty of time to spend in the Dunes, the best way to go is on the South Shore Line. Take fast, frequent South Shore Line trains direct to Tremont station, "Gateway to the Dunes"

81-minute scenic ride from downtown Chicago. Special round trip fare, $2.00 | Round trip fare from South Bend, $3.02 Special round trip fare Sat. and Sun., $1.75

Children under 5, if accompanied by adults, free; between 5 and 12 years, half fare

South Shore Line trains leave from six convenient I. C. suburban stations in Chicago:

Randolph St.   Roosevelt Rd. (Central Station)   Woodlawn (63d St.)
Van Buren St.   Hyde Park (53d St.)   Kensington

Randolph St.
Van Buren St.
Roosevelt Road (Central Station)
53rd St.
63rd St.
CHICAGO
Kensington
SOUTH
SHORE
GARY
THE DUNES
TREMONT
LAKE MICHIGAN
MICHIGAN CITY
SHORE
New Carlisle
SOUTH BEND
SOUTH   BEND   RAILROAD
AND

For train schedules, apply at the Outing and Recreation Bureau, or at any ticket office of the Chicago South Shore & South Bend Railroad (South Shore Line)

PROMOTIONAL BROCHURE OF SOUTH SHORE LINE. The advertising, promotional, and public relations efforts of the new South Shore Line management seemed inexhaustible. A public relations staff issued a continuing series of South Shore news stories to newspapers, magazines, and other publications. A carefully planned advertising program was developed in close coordination with the South Shore's traffic department. Newspaper advertising featured popular events or resorts available by South Shore trains, service changes, special rates, parlor and dining services, or general institutional copy. Window displays in principal stations were used to promote special events or attractions along the South Shore. Billboards, electric signs, and posters were used in the railway's outdoor advertising program. (Courtesy of Calumet Regional Archives of Indiana University Northwest, Gary, Indiana.)

What Is There to Do in the Indiana Dunes?

ENJOY Nature—that is the first thing to do in the Indiana Dunes. Enjoy the fresh air—the luxurious trees—the lovely flowers, plants and birds. Marvel at the wonders of Nature—the great sand hills, the shifting Dunes, the strange vegetation.

There are twenty-five miles of sandy, gradually-sloping Lake Michigan beach. Swim if you like. At Waverly Beach, within the State Park, is a bath house. There, for a small charge, you can change to swimming clothes and rent towels and lockers. You can rent a bathing suit, if you wish, for 50 cents.

Take along your lunch—or pick up a delicious box lunch, reasonably priced, at

Moonlight on the Beach

Tremont station of the South Shore Line. Throughout the vast State Park there are attractive places to eat a picnic lunch. There are numerous wells that provide pure drinking water. And there are crystal-clear springs which have been tested and marked by the State. Dunes Park is an ideal place for a camp-fire—a marshmallow or "weenie" roast.

Above all, hike about the Dunes. That is the only way to see them—the only way to become familiar with the beauties they possess. There's something new to see at every turn! Popular hiking trails are shown on the map printed herein. Take your camera—"shoot" the beauties of Nature.

To enjoy yourself in utmost comfort

Wear Your Old Clothes!

If you have a pair of high shoes, take them along

Three Popular Hiking Trails Through Dunes State Park

Pine Tree Trail

A hike that will consume the best part of a day, allowing ample time for "loafing" along the way.

If you intend to follow the Pine Tree Trail, it is a good plan to leave Chicago at about 9 a.m. on the South Shore Line, arriving at Tremont just 81 minutes later.

Leaving Tremont station, the trail leads directly north for about half a mile, where you

Cross Dunes Creek on rustic, wooden footbridge;

Turn to the northeast through a luxurious growth of trees, ferns, moss and flowers;

Then east along the foothills of the stationary dunes covered with dense forest vegetation;

You are now in the heart of a great, natural flower garden, the home of the cactus beds;

The foliage is thick, the sunlight filters through a gorgeous canopy of trees overhead;

The fragrant aroma of flowers fills the atmosphere;

At your right is Mt. Russell towering in the air;

The trail now bends to the southeast, where it borders the famous Tamarack swamp;

Here you see the peat bogs, which, in centuries, will be mined as coal for generations hence;

Here, too, you see the wild rice fields;

Now the trail starts upward at the foot of the migrating (or shifting) dunes behind the

A gigantic sand toboggan extending east for over half a mile, and gradually covering the forest and undergrowth of the swamp;

To the right you see "The Graveyard"—huge skeletons of trees that have been completely covered by the shifting dunes and are again coming to light as the dunes move along;

Here beneath the shade of protective trees is a good place to stop for lunch;

Then take up the trail once more, going directly north just a short distance to the lake;

Beautiful Lake Michigan, with its 25 miles of uninterrupted, sloping, sandy Dunes beach;

Now the trail goes west along the lake;

To the left are the mighty bluffs, rising abruptly from the beach;

Dotted here and there with a picturesque rustic cabin;

Now you view the blowouts and other sand formations from the wind-swept shores of the lake that gave them birth;

Opposite the highest point on the bluffs, where is located the Prairie Club House, the trail passes up the side of the cliff and to the south;

Once more you are in a heavily wooded section abounding with flowers;

To the right tower the mighty peaks of the three mountains, Mt. Tom, Mt. Jackson and Mt. Holden;

Gradually the trail descends to the foot of the ridges, back through rustic archways to the starting point.

A convenient, fast limited train on the South Shore Line takes you back home in time for the evening meal.

Hill Trail

Along the pathway are seen an endless array of beautiful flowers, ferns, moss and trees;

In just a short distance you come to the ridge of the bluffs that overlook Lake Michigan;

The trail follows the top of these hills to the foot of Mt. Holden;

You gradually ascend to the very top of this mountain;

After a rest on tree-covered Mt. Holden, the trail descends to the valley below;

Again you trek upward and ere long find yourself on the top of the highest point in the Dunes country, Mt. Tom;

From this point you can see three states, Indiana, Illinois and Michigan;

On a clear evening, the lights of the Wrigley Tower in downtown Chicago, nearly 50 miles away, are clearly visible;

Descending on the lake side of Mt. Tom, you come to Waverly Beach, where there are facilities for bathing;

Here, too, you find "Fish Johnson's," noted for its fish dinners;

The trail now leads back along the Dunes Creek, luxuriant with its growth of trees and plant life;

Shortly you find yourself at the starting point, ready to take a fast limited train on the South Shore Line back to your home.

Mt. Tom Trail

The Mt. Tom Trail leads directly to the highest point and one of the most popular spots in the Dunes country.

It passes at the foot of the three mountains, Mt. Jackson, Mt. Holden and Mt.

PROMOTIONAL BROCHURE OF SOUTH SHORE LINE. A Public Speaking Bureau organized by the South Shore supplied trained speakers for talks of a public relations nature. By far the most popular South Shore recreation spot, however, was the famous Indiana Dunes area along Lake Michigan between Gary and Michigan City, and the railway's greatest promotional efforts were directed to the development of traffic to the Dunes. The South Shore worked closely with the Indiana State Park Commission in efforts to protect the Dunes area from industrialization and to establish the 2,000-acre Indiana Dunes State Park. Plans were made to construct a spur track into the park, and the railway contributed $25,000 to a fund for the construction of a resort hotel and bath house in the Park at Waverly.

The attractions of the Dunes Park were regularly featured in South Shore posters, advertising, and promotional literature, such as a special map-folder which showed hiking trails in the Park. Advertising featured the slogan "See the Dunes Afoot" to encourage train riding rather than automobile travel to the Dunes. Special weekend and three-day excursion fares to the Dunes Park were offered. Construction of what was claimed to be the country's largest structural-steel ski-slide immediately adjacent to the railway at Ogden Dunes, 8-miles east of Gary, gave the South Shore still another recreational attraction. (Courtesy of Calumet Regional Archives of Indiana University Northwest, Gary, Indiana.)

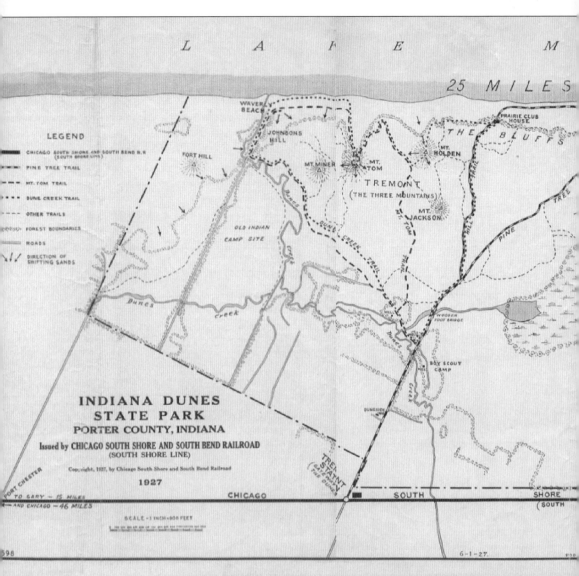

LAKE MICHIGAN

25 MILES

LEGEND

- CHICAGO SOUTH SHORE AND SOUTH BEND R.R. (SOUTH SHORE LINE)
- PINE TREE TRAIL
- MT. TOM TRAIL
- DUNE CREEK TRAIL
- OTHER TRAILS
- FOREST BOUNDARIES
- ROADS
- DIRECTION OF SHIFTING SANDS

WAVERLY BEACH

JOHNSONS HILL

FORT HILL

MT. MINER

MT. TOM

TREMONT
(THE THREE MOUNTAINS)

MT. JACKSON

PRAIRIE CLUB HOUSE

THE BLUFFS

MT. HOLDEN

OLD INDIAN CAMP SITE

Dunes Creek

WOODEN FOOT BRIDGE

BOY SCOUT CAMP

INDIANA DUNES
STATE PARK
PORTER COUNTY, INDIANA

Issued by CHICAGO SOUTH SHORE AND SOUTH BEND RAILROAD
(SOUTH SHORE LINE)

Copyright, 1927, by Chicago South Shore and South Bend Railroad

1927

FORT CHESTER

TO GARY — 15 MILES
AND CHICAGO — 46 MILES

CHICAGO   SOUTH   SHORE
(SOUTH

SCALE – 1 INCH = 600 FEET

6-1-27.

SEE THE DUNES VIA SOUTH SHORE L

INDIANA DUNES STATE PARK WALKING TRAILS BROCHURE PROVIDED BY SOUTH SHORE LINE. On July 27, 1927, the South Shore opened an Outing and Recreation Bureau and an Own Your Own Home Bureau in Chicago, which provided information concerning points of interest, resorts, vacation spots, and home sites along the interurban line, and were staffed to assist travelers in making all necessary arrangements. In 1927, some 550 agents of the Chicago Rapid Transit Company and the Illinois Central's suburban service were taken on a day's outing over South Shore's rail and motor coach lines. By gaining first-hand knowledge of South Shore services, reasoned the railway, these men would help sell its services to potential Chicago-area travelers. Particular effort went into the promotion of traffic to and from the resorts and recreation spots reached by the South Shore. Special party business in particular was vigorously and successfully promoted.

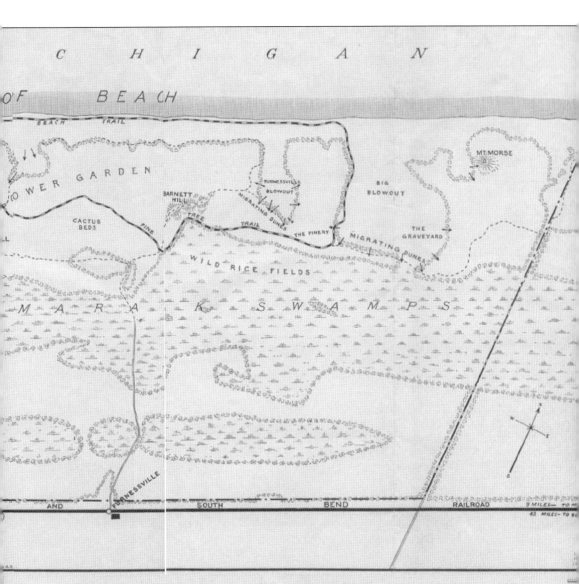

BEACH

OF

BEACH TRAIL

OWER GARDEN

CACTUS BEDS

BARNETT HILL

TURNESSVILLE BLOWOUT

MIGRATING DUNES

PINE TREE TRAIL

THE PINERY

MT. MORSE

BIG BLOWOUT

MIGRATING DUNES

THE GRAVEYARD

WILD RICE FIELDS

M A R A K S W A M P S

TURNESSVILLE

AND   SOUTH   BEND   RAILROAD   9 MILES — TO
                                                                                   43 MILES — TO SO

HIKE THROUGH THIS LAND OF CHARM

SAMUEL INSULL. In the American business world of the 1920s, Samuel Insull was a man of almost legendary reputation. Born in obscurity in London, England, in 1859, Sam Insull had risen to his prominence in the public utilities industry through a combination of immense energy and exceptional management ability.

At the age of 21, Insull came to the United States as private secretary to inventor Thomas A. Edison. Before Insull was 30, Edison sent him Schenectady, New York, to manage his new electrical manufacturing plant, which ultimately was to grow into the great General Electric Company. Leaving GE in 1892, Insull set out on his own in the then-infant central station power business, becoming president of the Chicago Edison Company. (Courtesy of Calumet Regional Archives of Indiana University Northwest, Gary, Indiana.)

Flowers and Plants

"In the Dunes, as nowhere else in the world," says Prof. Henry C. Cowles, of the University of Chicago, "there is a procession from April to October of beautiful flowers. Within a stone's throw of almost any spot one may find plants of the deserts and plants of rich woodlands, plants of the pine woods and plants of the swamps, plants of the oak woods and plants of the prairies."

Some of the plants and flowers of the Dunes are ferns, sand cherry, bearberry, hepatica, lupine, puccoon, phlox, trillium, bird's-foot violet, orchids, four species of lady's slipper, wild roses, columbine, twin flower, harebell, goat's rue, butterfly weed, flowering spurge, prickly pear cactus, goldenrod, aster, sunflowers, yellow geradias, gentians.

Trees

You will see, in the Dunes, giant white pines, white oaks with trunks nearly three feet through the center, black oaks, pin oaks, tulip trees, beech and poplars, junipers, sassafrass, ague trees, elms, silver maples, sugar maples, sand cherries, hickory, birch, sycamores, dogwoods, wild plums, wild crabapples, willows—a seemingly endless variety of trees and shrubs.

Birds

More than 300 varieties of birds have been seen in the Dunes. Among them are the kinglet, blue heron, wild canary, scarlet tanager, goldfinch, purple finch, wren, bobolink, meadow lark, cuckoo, dove, kildeer, mocking bird, thrush, phoebe, swallow, quail, sandpiper, owl, whip-poor-will, white and gray gull, wild duck, plover, thrasher, humming bird, oriole, indigo bunting, purple martin, bluebird, grackle, robin, warbler, to mention only a few.

Enjoy the Dunes at All Seasons

"To the query as to the best time to see the Dunes," says E. Stillman Bailey in his book on the Dunes, "I reply, the best time is at your own convenience. . . . The Dunes are fascinating at any and all times.

"Perhaps, as the 'old commuter' said to me recently, the Dunes are at their best in the spring; but the same enthusiast must have a short memory, for last fall he told me that the fall of the year is the best possible time.

"If you are warmly clad, you will welcome a trip to the Dunes even during the winter's snows and gales. If you are the Indian you think yourself, you will, on a summer day, take a fifteen-mile hike on the beach, hatless, and unconventionally plunge at your will into the lake for a refreshing swim, and later you may seek a resting spot to watch the sunset."

Winter hiking along the winding trails and stretches of even beach, and skiing on the hillsides, is a diversion that has gained wide popularity.

A Quiet Lily Pond in the Dunes

Where the Trail Leads Upward

See the "Shifting Dunes"

Many of the dunes, swept by wind, are moving constantly. You can see where whole forests are being covered up and blotted out by these shifting dunes. At other places you can see, poking through the dune sides, the skeletons of huge trees that have been covered by the shifting sand and are again being uncovered by the moving hills. It's a most weird and fascinating sight!

Like a Scene in Japan

Reminiscent of the Great Sahara

—and the Dunes Blowouts!

You will see, in the Indiana Dunes, huge "blowouts" where the wind has scooped out the sand and left the dune looking for all the world like the hollow of a giant dish—or like an amphitheater or a horseshoe. There is no end of interest in the sand formations. The dune sand is not gritty like ordinary sand—its texture is finer and softer—more like that of flour.

Shifting Dune Covering a Forest

A Picturesque Dunes Blowout

OUTING AND RECREATION BROCHURE. During the next several decades the Insull-managed company, which later became the giant Commonwealth Edison Company, pioneered much of the technology and the business methods which spurred the extraordinary growth of the electric power industry early in the 20th century, and became the cornerstone of a mammoth Insull-controlled public utilities empire that by 1930 was worth somewhere between $2 and $3 billion dollars; generated a tenth of the nation's electricity; and provided electric, gas, and transportation service to some 5,000 communities in 32 states.

Although his efforts had been largely in the public utilities field, Samuel Insull was by no means a newcomer to the electric railway industry when his Midland Utilities Company acquired control of the Chicago, Lake Shore and South Bend Railway in 1925. Indeed, Insull's interest in electric railways dated as far back as the early 1880s when he had participated in some of Thomas Edison's pioneering experiments in railroad electrification, and in later years he had come to believe that electric transportation would ultimately supplant all other means of mass transportation. (Photo courtesy of Calumet Regional Archives of Indiana University Northwest, Gary, Indiana.)

SOUTH SHORE TRAIN AT BEVERLY SHORES STATION. After the Chicago, Lake Shore and South Bend Railway was sold to Insull's Midland Utilities in 1925, both Insull and the South Shore Line supported the development of the Indiana Dunes State Park. The South Shore Line planned a spur line into the state park with "a rail terminal at the park entrance adjacent to a proposed hotel, bathing facilities, pier and dance pavilion." Construction of the hotel and bathhouse at the Indiana Dunes State Park was later assisted with a $25,000 gift from the railroad. Further, Insull personally assisted the state park development effort with a $200,000 loan to the Dunes Park Purchasing Board and a donation of land for the park entrance. The rail spur was never built, but its proposed alignment is now the extension of Indiana State Road 49 into the state park. (Photo courtesy of M. D. McCarter.)

SOUTH SHORE TRAIN ON BRIDGE AT BURNS DITCH. (Photo courtesy of M. D. McCarter.)

Baile's Cabin.

lish; the Chippewa and Pottawatomie, thanks mostly to Baile, kept faith with the colonists.

The Iroquois realized that they and their allies were outnumbered and called in tribes as far west as the Dakotas to lend support.

A great battle was impending. Prior to the fight, Baile sat in his cabin doorway and for two successive days watched a single file of Indians pass on their way to the battleground. They met the enemy southeast of Michigan City. The red allies of the colonies were defeated. But after an orderly retreat, they reorganized and met in a second battle east of Gary.

Here in the sand hills the Pottawatomies and their fellow warriors were victorious and completely routed the Iroquois. At the point of this combat, it is now possible to find broken bits of Indians weapons—stone tomahawks, chipped flint arrowheads and spear tips.

Today the cabins are kept in excellent condition by an order of Catholic Sisters known as the Nuns of Notre Dame. Visitors are always welcome and a visit to Baileytown, such a short distance from Chicago, will reveal many interesting relics of pioneer days.

The Outing and Recreation Bureau, 72 W. Adams St., Chicago, phone Randolph 8200, has a complete hike guide prepared on Baileytown and Mineral Springs. They will be glad to send you a copy.
Ask about South Shore Line train service to Baileytown and Mineral Springs. All trains leave Randolph St. I. C. Suburban station, and stop at Van Buren, Roosevelt Road, 53rd St., 63rd St., and Kensington.

BAILEYTOWN
AND
MINERAL SPRINGS

A Radio Talk
prepared and given by
C. Edward Thorney
Director
Outing and Recreation Bureau
72 W. ADAMS ST., CHICAGO

CHICAGO - SOUTH SHORE
& SOUTH BEND RAILROAD

BAILEYTOWN BROCHURE. Beginning in 1914, when the Chicago elevated system was unified under his control, Insull began acquiring widespread financial or management control of electric railway properties. By the time he assumed control of the South Shore, the Insull traction empire included an almost unbroken chain of interurban properties extending from Milwaukee to Louisville, and the electric railway trade press was giving serious attention to rumors that a single giant Insull interurban system was in the making.

Intriguing as the prospects of through interurban operation over such a system might have been, the Insull interest in the South Shore Line stemmed from more realistic considerations. Despite the dismal financial performance of the predecessor Chicago, Lake Shore and South Bend, the region served by the South Shore Line remained one of exceptionally great promise for an interurban railway. The South Shore Line provided a direct link between Chicago and several of the largest cities in Indiana, and between 1907 and 1925 the population in the area directly tributary to the railway had more than doubled, from 175,000 to 390,000. (Photo courtesy of Calumet Regional Archives of Indiana University Northwest, Gary, Indiana.)

TANDING silhouetted against a Hoosier sky is a rough-hewn cross, beneath which lie the bodies of two revered pioneers of northern Indiana, the French-Canadian Baile and his English wife. Set back in the trees a short distance from the old Detroit Plank Road at Baileytown, southeast from Chicago on Lake Michigan, are the log cabins built by the trader after he had worked his way into the forests.

Baileytown has never lost its glamour of true American romance. Once it was the western frontier of the rapidly expanding colonies. It is today reminiscent of Indian warfare, massacres, trail blazing and stage coach roads.

Baile the Frontiersman

The life of the frontiersman, Baile, as a fur trader was typical of the lives of other brave men who made the Middle West possible for settlement. He was born of French parents in 1783 and upon reaching young manhood established himself in the trading post at Mackinac Island.

In his daily dealings with the Indians of the lakes tribes, he familiarized himself with their customs. Better than that, through his fairness and sympathy, he won their friendship and love.

One day an Indian chief and his squaw, accompanied by a fair skinned maiden, appeared at his trading store. Baile gained their confidence and learned that she was the daughter of an aristocratic English family of Detroit. She had been kidnapped in childhood by a roving band of Chippewa Indians. The chief was the leader of the band and intended to hold the child as a hostage. He and his squaw became attached to the girl and adopted her into their tribe and later into their own family. She had been raised as an Indian princess.

Several years of courtship followed Baile's first acquaintance with the white girl and finally they were married. In this little trading post on Mackinac Island their first child was born—and died. The baby was buried under a tree that today still stands outside the Fort at Mackinac Island.

The young couple were heartbroken. Baile and his wife determined to enter the rich fur country of the lower Lake Michigan region. He stood in high favor with the British Commissioners in control of the country and obtained a land grant giving Indian territory at the south end of the Lake.

In a canoe, carrying all their worldly possessions, he and his wife paddled down Lake Michigan from Mackinac Island and after two months selected a site overlooking the Calumet River, where today is Mineral Springs.

The Baile Memorial.

Baile named the country after the Indian pipe of peace, the Calumet. The lower Lake Michigan region is still known as the Calumet Region. Baile discovered the many springs of the territory which are now known for their medicinal properties.

Some time after their settlement along the river, Baile and his wife felt the need of white companions and returned to Mackinac Island. Then, too, they had decided to bring the body of their baby to a resting place near their Calumet home, and this they did.

Rough country separated their clearings from the lake shore and in order to reach its waters, it was necessary to construct a road through woods and dunes. This was about the time of the settlement of Fort Dearborn.

The American and the British carried on a continual guerilla warfare through the northwest. Detachments of Red Coats overran the country. This hostility reached such proportions that it was imperative that the Bailes seek haven in Detroit, but shortly after they had started overland, English raiders overtook them. Although most of the party escaped, Mrs. Baile was taken captive and carried into Wisconsin.

The Patriot

Baile, with friendly Indians, scoured the country and aroused allied Indians to the American cause. Things were getting so hot for the British they ultimately released Mrs. Baile and she returned to her family in Baileytown.

A period of comparative inactivity followed during which Baile surveyed the entire area between his home and the mouth of the Calumet River. In his report to the American colonial government he suggested the possibility of a future waterway development. He was the first to lay out a definite waterways program for the Middle West.

But the Indians were restless. Great Britain finally succeeded in fomenting enmity between the various tribes. The Ottawa and Iroquois sided with the Eng-

BAILEYTOWN BROCHURE. Sam Insull's Midlands Utility Company believed that it could create business through suburban development by providing superior electric transportation. To that end, by 1926 Insull had acquired the South Shore Line as well as the other two heavy-duty interurban railroads radiating from Chicago, the Chicago North Shore and Milwaukee (North Shore Line) and the Chicago Aurora and Elgin. Insull's investment in interurban railroads appeared to be ill-timed. Not only did Insull underestimate the impact of the automobile on railroad ridership, he could not foresee the Depression and its impact on land development. As the economy continued to thrive, however, the Insull-owned interurban railroads jointly created the Outing and Recreation and Own Your Own Home bureaus on June 27, 1927. Supporting the work of the bureaus, the previously launched poster campaign was more than just a colorful footnote in the history of Insull's interurban railroads. Through the poster art, Insull hoped to develop northwest Indiana. (Photo courtesy of Calumet Regional Archives of Indiana University Northwest, Gary, Indiana.)

CHICAGO, LAKE SHORE AND SOUTH BEND WOODEN PASSENGER CARS, BEFORE THE INSULL TAKEOVER, MILLER STATION. Before the Insull management took charge of the South Shore Line, little effort was made to coordinate the development of the railway with the economic development of the Region. Any effort that might have been made was hampered by the poor financial performance of the South Shore Line's predecessor, the Chicago, Lake Shore and South Bend Railway. The Chicago, Lake Shore and South Bend did play some role in developing northwest Indiana, however, by providing excursions to the Dunes for the Prairie Club of Chicago. The completion of the Chicago, Lake Shore and South Bend Railway in 1908 as being "perhaps the most important of all . . . in [rapidly increasing] interest in the dunes among artists and writers." Spurred by the access to the Dunes created by the Chicago, Lake Shore and South Bend Railway, the Prairie Club and National Dunes Park Association began a lobbying effort, resulting in the establishment of the Indiana Dunes State Park in 1925. (Photos courtesy of M.C. McCarter.)

PROMOTIONAL PIECES. The South Shore Line was the only railroad serving the Dunes east of what was then called Dune Park (where Bethlehem Steel located in 1964), and the railroad took full advantage of it. The South Shore Line publicity department described its Dunes promotional efforts as have "exploited [the Dunes] to a great degree." The Outing and Recreation Bureau's Dunes promotional campaign included newspaper advertising trumpeting the dunes as the place "Where Wilderness is King," pamphlets stressing that Duneland is "Chicago's favorite playground," and trail guides of the State Park that described "The Dunes—What they are—What to do there—And how to reach them conveniently and safely." It is no coincidence that 23 of the 38 known surviving South Shore Line posters feature recreation in the Dunes. (Courtesy of Calumet Regional Archives of Indiana University Northwest, Gary, Indiana.)

The DUNES

VISIT the Dunes this season! See them afoot, for the charm of the old beautiful trails, the big trees and flower fields, the great sand mountains and perfect beach, is mostly for those who hike. To discover rainbows of brilliant birds; drowsy lagoons in the forests; shady valleys in which to spread a lunch cloth; dune tops and a glimpse of Chicago across Lake Michigan, or a white paradise of snow,—that will be the Dunes.

On a sunny day you can step from a South Shore Line train into the Kingdom of Romance in Indiana Dunes State Park. Go once—rigged up in your outing togs, with a camera and a lunch along—and you'll be going every chance you have.

DUNES PARK EXCURSION. Immediately east of the state park in 1929 were the subdivisions of the Fred'k H. Bartlett Realty Co.: Beverly Shores, Lake Shore, North Shore Beach, and South Shore Acres, the largest lakefront development ever in Chicagoland. Once the South Shore Line had introduced visitors to the beauty of the Indiana Dunes, perhaps they would like to have a piece of the wilderness all to themselves—Chicago's Largest Real Estate Operator could get it for them. And once they have built their suburban dream homes among the dunes, they could conveniently travel to downtown Chicago from one of two new $15,000 South Shore Line stations. Their ride would be aboard modern "electrically-operated trains [that] embody all the refinements and comforts of steam railroad Pullman car travel–without the unpleasant dirt, dust, and cinders," as the advertising explained. Clearly the South Shore Line wanted Chicagoans to see the Dunes through the posters, come to Indiana for recreation, and then build their suburban homes and stay. In theory, through the medium of the posters, the promotional campaign of the Outing and Recreation Bureau and the Own Your Own Home Bureau could transform an occasional rider out to tour the Dunes into a regular commuter. (Courtesy of Calumet Regional Archives of Indiana University Northwest, Gary, Indiana.)

DOWNTOWN CHICAGO. The present South Shore company was organized in June 1925, by Samuel Insull, who purchased the old company at a receivership sale. Under his direction a complete rehabilitation program was instituted. Rails and ties were replaced, the overhead catenary system was reconstructed, new passenger cars were added and a few freight locomotives were purchased. A change in voltage powering the line also enabled it to carry passengers directly into the heart of Chicago. This latter improvement is listed by company officials as the greatest single factor in the success of the line. (Photo courtesy of M.D. McCarter.)

CHICAGO, LAKE SHORE AND SOUTH BEND WOODEN CARS. Prior to the Samuel Insull takeover of the Chicago, Lake Shore and South Bend Railroad through his Midland Utilities Company, passengers were not able to go from Indiana to downtown Chicago without a change of trains or a change to a steam engine at or near the state line of Indiana and Illinois. However, after Insull's acquisition of Chicago, Lake Shore and South Bend, he electrified the Illinois Central urban line in Chicago, which provided the link-up without requiring passengers to change trains or locomotives. (Photo courtesy of M.D. McCarter.)

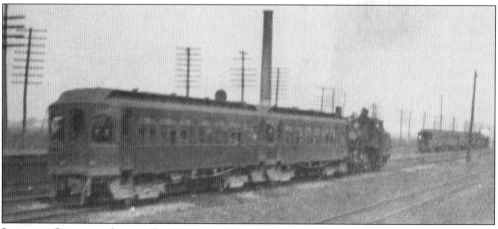

ILLINOIS CENTRAL STEAM ENGINE AT KENSINGTON, WITH CHICAGO, LAKE SHORE AND SOUTH BEND PASSENGER CARS. (Photo courtesy of M.D. McCarter.)

LITHOGRAPHED POSTERS. One of the most notable features of the South Shore advertising program was the railway's series of distinguished lithographed posters, which were published regularly for exhibition in company stations, on Chicago "L" platforms, and in schools and libraries in South Shore territory. Designed by prominent Chicago artists, the poster series won wide distinction for its high artistic standards. One, "Homeward Bound by South Shore Line," by artist Oscar Rabe Hanson, won both the Art Directors Club and Baron Collier medals at the sixth annual exhibition of advertising art at the Art Center in New York City in 1927.

The posters were designed in an idealistic and stylized manner that appealed to discerning Chicagoans. The message was simple: by riding this railroad you could choose the perfect vacation spot, and it was only minutes away. (Courtesy of Posters Plus, Chicago, Illinois.)

Published Monthly for Patrons of the Chicago South Shore and South Bend Railroad

VOL. 4　　　　　　SEPTEMBER, 1929　　　　　　No. 11

Plan to Spend $250,000 on Dunes Park

THE State of Indiana, which for some time has been planning extensive improvements in Indiana Dunes State Park, will start work on a $250,000 construction program this fall.

This is the statement of Richard C. Lieber, director of the state department of conservation, made recently on a visit to Gary.

Included in the development plans are the diversion of Fort creek at Waverly beach, construction on the beach of a large bathing pavilion, community mart and recreation building combined, a comfort station and rest rooms adjacent to the bathing pavilion, and other projects.

Will Have Stores

According to Col. Lieber, the bathhouse, to be started October 1, will be 170 by 60 feet, two stories high, and of cement and stone. The first floor will contain a large soft drink parlor and grill room, and two stores for dispensing both novelty goods and groceries. The second floor will contain dressing rooms for bathers. The flat roof, covered with beach sand, will be used for promenading and as a playground for small children.

"It is the policy of the state conservation department to restore the park to its primeval state as it was when the red man made the original trails and as it was when Father Marquette first glimpsed the wonderful glory of the dune region," Col. Lieber said. "There will be no motor drive along the beach and there will be no motor drives through the park. The old Indian trails and pioneer roads will be maintained as they were a century ago."

(Continued on Page 7)

TWO-DINER TRAINS
SET NEW PRECEDENT

During August and through Labor Day two dining cars were operated on each of three South Shore Line limited train runs, the first regular service of this kind ever offered on an American electric railway.

Every Friday the St. Joe Valley Limited, out of Randolph St., Chicago, at 5:15 P. M., has been carrying two dining cars. Every Saturday noon, the Indiana Limited, leaving Randolph St. station at 12 o'clock, likewise has had two diners attached. Every Monday morning, the Fort Dearborn Limited, Chicago-bound flyer leaving South Bend at 7:05 A. M., Michigan City at 7:48 A. M., daylight saving time, also has been a double diner train. All these trains carry the new parlor cars in addition.

For the benefit of Michigan City patrons, the second diner on the Monday morning train was placed in front of the station, Eleventh St. between Franklin and Pine, at 7:30 A. M., 18 minutes before leaving time, with breakfast ready.

At the same time two new dining car trains were announced, for service during the balance of the summer. These are the Chicago Limited leaving Michigan City for Chicago at

MAGAZINES. Promotional materials printed and distributed by the South Shore included folders, blotters, booklets, and other literature featuring the railway's services or points of interest. An eight-page monthly magazine, *South Shore Lines*, was distributed to the public in trains and stations, or by mail.

The South Shore magazines were intended to pique the interest, curiosity, and pocket books of people in the Chicago and outlying areas to encourage them to vacation in the diverse regions along the train's route.

Scenes of frolicking beach-goers in Lake Michigan, tastefully dressed skiers on pristine slopes, picturesque rural landscapes, and gleaming steel mill smoke-stacks were common subjects. (Courtesy of Calumet Regional Archives of Indiana University Northwest, Gary, Indiana.)

Three

BEVERLY SHORES: EARLY DEVELOPMENT

FREDERICK BARTLETT ADMINISTRATION

FIRST BEACHSIDE HOME, 1929. The influence of 1920s Florida resorts on Beverly Shores' development is most evident in the architectural forms chosen to define its image. Bartlett planned to build a series of public buildings, as well as a number of strategically-placed houses, in the Mediterranean Revival style, and to use these forms in his advertising to create a visual image for his resort. Each of these buildings was essentially a modern utilitarian structure, yet they shared a common palette of exterior materials and forms which were to have coalesced into a clear community architectural character if built in sufficient numbers. (Photo courtesy of Beverly Shores Museum and Art Gallery, Inc., Beverly Shores, Indiana.)

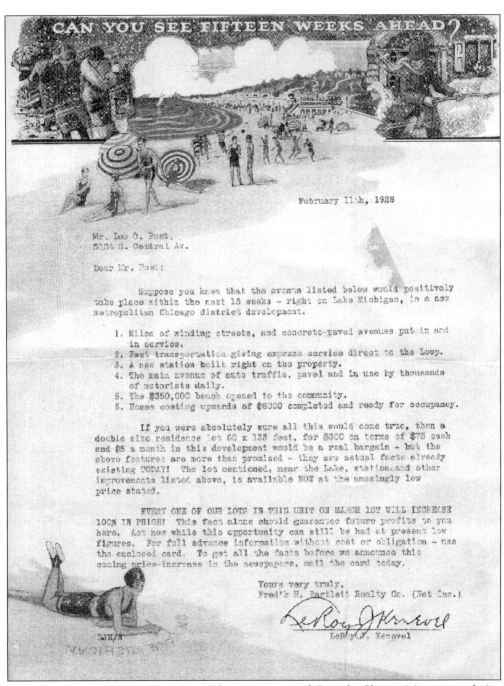

CAN YOU SEE FIFTEEN WEEKS AHEAD?

February 11th, 1928

Mr. Leo O. Post,
5154 S. Central Av.

Dear Mr. Post:

Suppose you knew that the events listed below would positively take place within the next 15 weeks - right on Lake Michigan, in a new metropolitan Chicago district development.

1. Miles of winding streets, and concrete-paved avenues put in and in service.
2. Fast transportation giving express service direct to the Loop.
3. A new station built right on the property.
4. The main avenue of auto traffic, paved and in use by thousands of motorists daily.
5. The $350,000 beach opened to the community.
6. Homes costing upwards of $6000 completed and ready for occupancy.

If you were absolutely sure all this would come true, then a double size residence lot 60 x 133 feet, for $300 on terms of $75 cash and $5 a month in this development would be a real bargain - but the above features are more than promised - they are actual facts already existing TODAY! The lot mentioned, near the Lake, station and other improvements listed above, is available NOW at the amazingly low price stated.

EVERY ONE OF OUR LOTS IN THIS UNIT ON MARCH 1ST WILL INCREASE 100% IN PRICE! This fact alone should guarantee future profits to you here. Act now while this opportunity can still be had at present low figures. For full advance information without cost or obligation - use the enclosed card. To get all the facts before we announce this coming price-increase in the newspapers, mail the card today.

Yours very truly,
Fred'k H. Bartlett Realty Co. (Not Inc.)

LeRoy J. Knavel

LeRoy J. Knavel

LJK/N

BARTLETT PROMOTIONAL LETTER. (Photo courtesy of Beverly Shores Museum and Art Gallery, Inc., Beverly Shores, Indiana.)

BARTLETT SALESMEN AT BEVERLY SHORES, 1933. Pictured, from left to right, unknown; Bert Laudermilk; John Turek; unknown; Harry Selinski; Charles Selinski; and unknowns. Frederick Bartlett promoted Beverly Shores with many of the methods perfected by Florida's developers. He employed salesmen to comb South Chicago's ethnic neighborhoods looking for relatively affluent individuals interested in escaping their crowded industrial environment. After locating interested parties, the developer transported them on daily South Shore trains specially painted in red, white, and blue, and labeled "Bartlett Specials," which carried them from neighborhood interurban stops to the Beverly Shores station. When a prospective buyer arrived at the South Shore station, a salesman immediately ushered them to a black Packard which carried them on a tour of the resort. This tour ended with a complimentary meal where free drinks were purported to have boosted the sale of property. (Photo courtesy of Beverly Shores Museum and Art Gallery, Inc., Beverly Shores, Indiana.)

THE FIRST HOME ON LAKE FRONT DRIVE, 1929. On July 22, 1929, Frederick Bartlett proclaimed that he had 1,400 acres of land to be developed on the shores of Lake Michigan, with 2 miles of shoreland, to be a combination of a suburban town and lakeside resort development.

Bartlett contracted for engineering and surveying to the A.J. Silander Co. of Chicago, and the paving of Broadway within the 100 feet of dedicated street from the Dunes Highway to Lake Front Drive to H.B. Hutchingson Co. of Michigan City.

Also in 1929, H.B. Olney Co. of East Chicago was contracted to build 50 homes as a nucleus of a residential district in Beverly Shores, as announced by Robert Bartlett, then general manager and vice president of the Frederick Bartlett Realty Co.

Leo Post was contracted to build the first structures in Beverly Shores, starting with the South Shore train station in 1929, adopting the Mediterranean Revival style designed by architect Arthur U. Gerber. Post was further contracted to build the Administration Building, Post Office, Country Club Building, and many Mediterranean Revival homes designed by Fred Mertz, as illustrated in the Bartlett Plan Book of the so-called *A-B-C-D-E Homes*. Many other builders also participated in building homes in Beverly Shores. (Photo courtesy of Beverly Shores Museum and Art Gallery, Inc., Beverly Shores, Indiana.)

BROADWAY SOUTH SHORE LINE STATION. The 1929 South Shore train station on Broadway was one of two such stations built in Beverly Shores in conjunction with the interurban company. Its distinctive Spanish character was once shared by several other stations on Insull's lines, but today it remains the sole structure of this type still in use. This small Mediterranean Revival station/ticket vendor's residence was designed by Chicago Architect Arthur U. Gerber. It consists of a passenger waiting room on the right and on the left, the former ticket vendor's residence. This building is embellished with a tall stucco chimney capped with a barrel tile roof, as well as an arched front porch surrounded by a patio and leading to an arched front door. The building's casement windows, French doors, and barrel tile roof strengthen the station's Spanish character. A large neon sign mounted on the station's roof still boldly announces "Beverly Shores" to South Shore Line passengers.(Photo courtesy of Beverly Shores Museum and Art Gallery, Inc., Beverly Shores, Indiana.)

Former Central Avenue South Shore Line Station. This latest enterprise of the Bartlett Company is the firm's third Lake Michigan waterfront development and plans indicate it will be the greatest of the three. The success of Lake Shore and of North Shore Beach, the first two, totaling more than $15 million in reservations, proves the demand for lake frontage is growing and played an important part in the firm's determination to launch its third great waterfront project.

To make possible the opening of a town site of such magnitude on the lake front it was necessary to purchase the 2,000 acres held intact for many years by the Wells estate. One half of this holding was acquired by the state of Indiana for Dunes Park. The other 1,000 acres were acquired by the Bartlett interests who have since acquired 400 acres more, bringing the total area of their project to its present size. (Photo courtesy of Beverly Shores Museum and Art Gallery, Inc., Beverly Shores, Indiana.)

ADMINISTRATION BUILDING. The administration building was constructed on the west side of Broadway across from the train station, and remains a distinctly Spanish, yet functional structure. It is a rectangular, one-story, beige brick building with an arched center entrance at the base of a two-story tower. Although this building has a flat roof surrounded by a parapet wall, its front parapet is recessed and is veneered with a short sloping clay tile roof. The tower is also roofed in tile, and has paired arched openings each supported by twisted Spanish columns and enclosed by cast iron railings. The building's large front windows have always been commercial in nature. This building was constructed as the reception and administration center of the development, and was designed to reinforce the resort's marketed image while functioning as a practical office structure. (Photo courtesy of Beverly Shores Museum and Art Gallery, Inc., Beverly Shores, Indiana.)

COUNTRY CLUB BUILDING. Bartlett strengthened upscale buyers' attraction to his development by constructing an 18-hole golf course and club house as the southern termination of Broadway, just across the railroad tracks and Highway 12 from the town's center. The clubhouse carried on the town's architectural theme by displaying arched windows and open loggias, stucco cladding, and a barrel tile roof. (Photo courtesy of Beverly Shores Museum and Art Gallery, Inc., Beverly Shores, Indiana.)

INTERIOR VIEWS OF COUNTRY CLUB BUILDING. The decision to develop Beverly Shores was reached by the firm after long consideration and a thorough real estate market analysis that revealed a growing demand and an acute necessity for this type of suburban town site in the metropolitan Chicago area.

"Recent surveys showing a population increase of approximately 60,000 annually in metropolitan Chicago also show that this influx of people is making Lake Michigan the most popular of the Great Lakes," said Mr. Robert Bartlett, general manager and vice-president of the firm, commenting on the compiled research data. "Attendance at Chicago's beaches is creating an overcrowded condition that is not being met be additional beach lands." (Photo courtesy of Beverly Shores Museum and Art Gallery, Inc., Beverly Shores, Indiana.)

BARTLETT PLAN BOOK. Although many lots were sold in Bartlett's first Beverly Shores marketing drive, only about 25 houses were actually constructed before 1935. These houses were built in the Mediterranean Revival style of the public buildings according to plans chosen by their owners from a special plan book published by Bartlett. This book contained detailed descriptions about how the Beverly Shores Construction Company erected houses and the quality materials they used. This plan book closely resembled the promotional literature used by today's developers, both carefully crafting an image of quality and style for completely unbuilt developments. The book's cover illustration portrays a scenic duneland landscape dotted with elegant Spanish villas and a convertible automobile winding its way down a curved road to a large public beach bordering the expanse of Lake Michigan. (Photo courtesy of Beverly Shores Museum and Art Gallery, Inc., Beverly Shores, Indiana.)

HOW BEVERLY SHORES HOME
ARE BUILT
A Story of Construction

HARMONY in home-building is the keynote of the construction program under way in Beverly Shores of Lake Michigan, metropolitan Chicago's latest and greatest lake front development.

Unlike the usual extensive building projects where row after row of houses, as alike as sardines in a can, assail the eye, this is a place where every home under construction is designed to conform with the natural beauty of the property as well as to provide a substantial, practical home. Monotonous repetition is avoided. The architectural plan being followed is resulting in the erection of distinctly individual residences, seaside villas, and model

homes worthy of Chicago's finest suburban sites along her precious, limited Lake Michigan shoreline.

Each home is planned to utilize to greatest advantage the particular site upon which it is built, thus enhancing values and presenting an architectural beauty that is generally not found in so-called "stock" houses. Every problem of the process of construction was taken up step by step by the architectural department in a way that is making Beverly Shores homes the most modern, convenient, and desirable dwellings possible for homeowners to possess today.

INTRODUCTION OF
HOUSE PLAN BOOK.
(Photo courtesy of
Beverly Shores
Museum and Art
Gallery, Inc.,
Beverly Shores,
Indiana.)

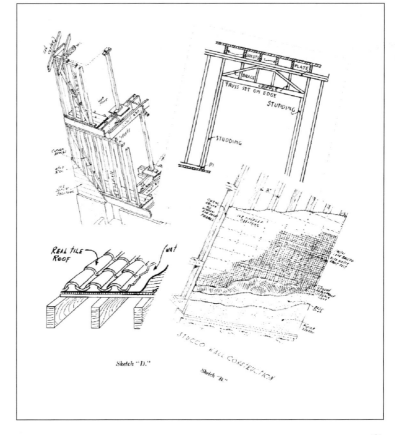

61

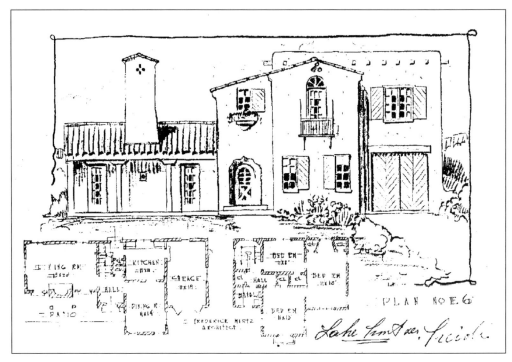

UNDER CONSTRUCTION From the plan book, drawing of Plan No. E6, which is shown under construction at left in the photo. Plan No. E7, also under construction, is at right in the photo. These two homes were the first to be built on the beach side of Lake Front Drive and were probably used as Bartlett's model display homes. (Photo courtesy of Beverly Shores Museum and Art Gallery, Inc., Beverly Shores, Indiana.)

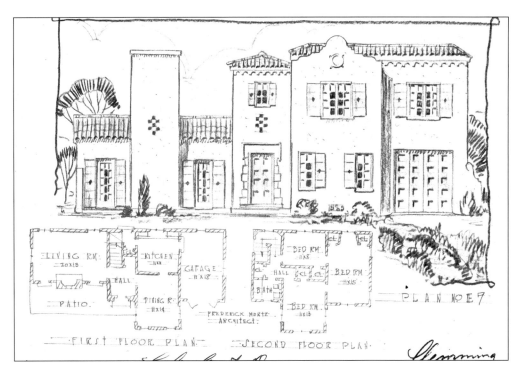

Within the drawing:

LIVING RM. 20x13 · KITCHEN 11x8 · GARAGE 11x18

HALL · PATIO · DINING R. 11x14

BED RM. 11x8 · BED RM. 11x15 · BED RM. 11x13 · HALL · BATH

FREDERICK MERTZ ARCHITECT

PLAN NO E7

FIRST FLOOR PLAN · SECOND FLOOR PLAN

PLAN NO. E7. The photo of the house shown is a view of its rear, which faces toward the lakefront. This house is also shown in a photo on the previous page, under construction. It is shown at the far right of photograph. (Photo courtesy of Indiana Dunes National Lakeshore, Porter, Indiana.)

PLAN NO. E10. The Mediterranean Revival houses illustrated in the plan book and built in the first growth phase were mostly small cottages scattered along the curvilinear streets in the dunes adjacent to Broadway. These houses were designed by the architect Frederick Mertz in a style which reflects the architectural traits of Florida's resorts, such as strong indoor/outdoor transitional space (created by frequent use of double French doors.), arcaded windows leading from high-ceilinged living rooms to patios, and floor plans which were usually only one room deep. These houses ranged from modest one- and two-bedroom homes, to large in size and from $3,500 to $6,000 in price. Details such as authentic Spanish tile, arched windows, wrought iron, and textured stucco all contributed to this Florida resort flavor. The villas constructed closer to the lake tended to be larger, some of them carefully built into the sides of the dunes to create interesting double-volume living spaces facing the lake vistas. (Photo courtesy of Beverly Shores Museum and Art Gallery, Inc., Beverly Shores, Indiana.)

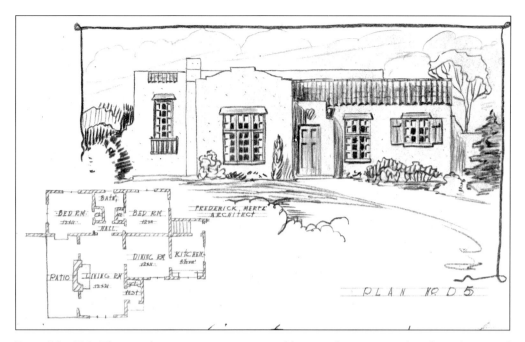

PLAN No. D5. These early structures were serviced by an infrastructure of roads, utilities, and public parks installed by the developer in order to attract further development. Bartlett seems to have paved the major access roads such as Broadway soon after starting the resort. These roads were of high-quality, reinforced-concrete construction, and many are still in use today. A limited number of concrete light standards were erected along these roads. Two public areas, an expansive beach and a small park in the dunes, also seem to have originated during this time. The only utility network installed in the town was a system of electric power lines, installed as part of the cooperative effort with Samuel Insull. Each structure was constructed with its own motorized well and septic system, and if heating or cooking gas was demanded, it was supplied through bottled propane. (Photo courtesy of Beverly Shores Museum and Art Gallery, Inc., Beverly Shores, Indiana.)

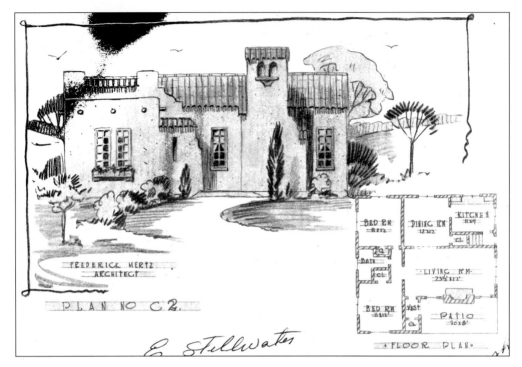

FREDERICK MERTZ
ARCHITECT

PLAN NO C2.

E. Stillwater

BED RM 11x12	DINING RM 12x12	KITCHEN 11x9
BATH		
	LIVING RM 23½x12	
BED RM 11x12	VEST	PATIO 20x8

• FLOOR PLAN •

PLAN No. C2. As previously mentioned, the land on which Beverly Shores was established, along with the rest of Indiana's Lake Michigan shoreline, was originally a complex environment of sandy beaches and dunes, swampy marshes, and dense woods. Although Indiana became a state in 1816, this land legally remained Indian territory until the expulsion of the Potawatomi tribe in 1838. Soon after, a Michigan City banker and businessman named Chauncy Blair purchased the large tract of land, which stretched westward from Michigan City to Tremont, from the Federal Government. (Photo courtesy of Beverly Shores Museum and Art Gallery, Inc., Beverly Shores, Indiana.)

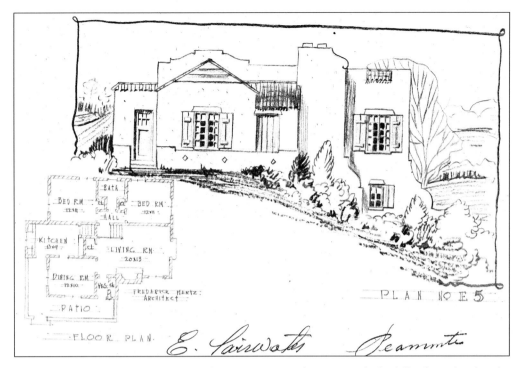

PLAN NO. E5. This land's physical characteristics made it particularly difficult to develop for agricultural or commercial use in the 1800s, and it remained largely as a wilderness disturbed only by land traffic passing through on its way to Chicago. Michigan City served as the termination of westward roads leading to Chicago from southern Indiana and Lake Erie, from which these roads combined into a difficult path through the dunelands. (Photo courtesy of Beverly Shores Museum and Art Gallery, Inc., Beverly Shores, Indiana.)

PLAN NO. E8. At first this path ran on the open sandy beach, but the unpredictability of the shoreline and the softness of the sand soon motivated the construction of an inland road. This first road ran behind the dunes, and was thus subject to flooding and deep mud in this marshy area. In spite of its use as a transport route, the natural difficulties of the duneland area precluded significant early development beyond the scattered huts of trappers and a few isolated farms. (Photo courtesy of Beverly Shores Museum and Art Gallery, Inc., Beverly Shores, Indiana.)

PLAN NO. E2.

FLOOR PLAN

Greatwater   *Wollet*

PLAN NO. E2. In 1901, Blair sold the Beverly Shores site to a syndicate of British interests called the Eastern Indiana Company. This syndicate employed Stanford A. White, director of the Chicago Board of Trade, as their local agent to carry out ambitious plans for their property. White employed a resident caretaker to oversee the site, who, with his family, became the first permanent residents of what would become Beverly Shores. The syndicate experimented with lumbering, grazing cattle, harvesting berries, and general farming, but could find no profitable use for the land. (Photo courtesy of Beverly Shores Museum and Art Gallery, Inc., Beverly Shores, Indiana.)

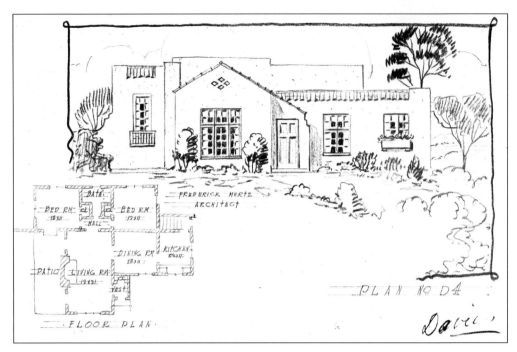

PLAN NO. D4. By the 1920s, the British group was looking for a buyer for their property. One interested party was the Bethlehem Steel Corporation, which eventually located its massive steel plant at nearby Burns Harbor in the 1960s. However, the continued natural character of this area was ensured when the State of Indiana bought the western portion of this land for use as the Indiana Dunes State Park. In 1927, the Eastern Indiana Company sold the eastern half of their property to the Chicago real estate developer, Frederick Bartlett. (Photo courtesy of Beverly Shores Museum and Art Gallery, Inc., Beverly Shores, Indiana.)

PLAN NO. C10. Frederick Bartlett was a developer who was accustomed to planning on a large scale. After naming his proposed resort after his daughter Beverly, he proceeded to create a comprehensive design for its development. Bartlett was very aware of the latest resort developments recently created in Florida through their publicity in the national media, and he was wealthy enough to have frequented them himself. Consequently, the plan he promoted for his new resort bore a strong resemblance to Mizner's resorts, as well as the influence of Olmsteadean suburban development of Riverside, Illinois. (Photo courtesy of Beverly Shores Museum and Art Gallery, Inc., Beverly Shores, Indiana.)

The following text and labels appear within the architectural drawing:

KITCHEN 9x10

BED RM 12½x11

CL

DINING RM 12x11¼

BATH

CL

BED RM 12½x11

FREDERICK MERTZ ARCHITECT

LIVING RM 12x21

VEST

CL

PLAN NO C9

FLOOR PLAN

PLAN NO. C9. Bartlett retained surveyors to develop the original plat of Beverly Shores, but it is evident that its planner set out to create a suburban type of development centering on an interurban station and immediately directing movement toward the lake. Just as in Boca Raton, a major boulevard extended straight from the South Shore interurban station northward through a commercial/administrative center, eventually terminating at a public beach and casino site. This main street, called Broadway, was flanked on both sides by a system of curvilinear residential streets which progressed from a loose grid in the flat marshland behind the dunes, to a maze of twisting lanes in the steep hills and valleys of the lakefront dunes. (Photo courtesy of Beverly Shores Museum and Art Gallery, Inc., Beverly Shores, Indiana.)

PLAN NO. C7. The straight access of Broadway was supplemented by linear secondary streets flanking Broadway on the east and west boundaries of the site, as well as by a lakefront road and a major east-west cross street behind the dunes called Beverly Drive. It was logical for Beverly Shores to be designed in relation to its rail access since this was the easiest and most rapid means of reaching the resort from South Chicago. However, the planner also acknowledged the growing importance of the motor car by creating three strong road entries to the town from Highway 12 (Dunes Highway), which ran along the south boundary of the development. (Photo courtesy of Beverly Shores Museum and Art Gallery, Inc., Beverly Shores, Indiana.)

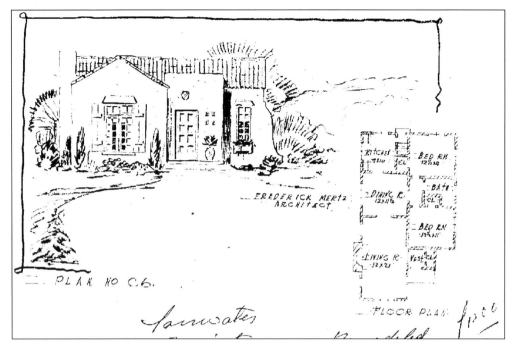

PLAN NO. C6. From its founding in the 1830s, Chicago has been a city of rampant land speculation. Chicagoans, from the upper to the lower-middle classes, have exhibited a long tradition of purchasing residential lots far beyond the existing city boundaries in order to resell them when prices rose. This trend accelerated as improved transportation opened up previously rural land to commuters. (Photo courtesy of Beverly Shores Museum and Art Gallery, Inc., Beverly Shores, Indiana.)

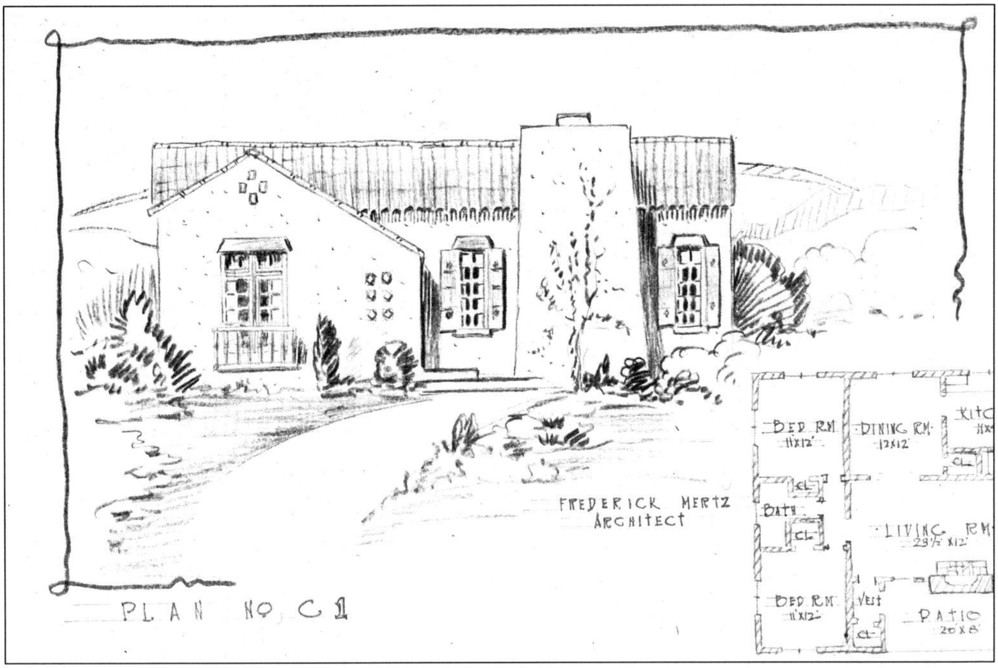
FREDERICK MERTZ
ARCHITECT
PLAN NO C1
BED RM
DINING RM
12x12
BATH
LIVING RM
BED RM
VEST
PATIO
20x8

PLAN NO. C1. On the south side of Chicago, the railroad lines spawned short-lived suburbs which spread a thin layer of residents over the area soon after the Civil War. However, the flat topography and easy lake access quickly attracted dense industrial development to the area, driving out the early suburbs. By 1890, South Chicago was a district of dense company towns clustered between massive heavy manufacturing facilities. (Photo courtesy of Beverly Shores Museum and Art Gallery, Inc., Beverly Shores, Indiana.)

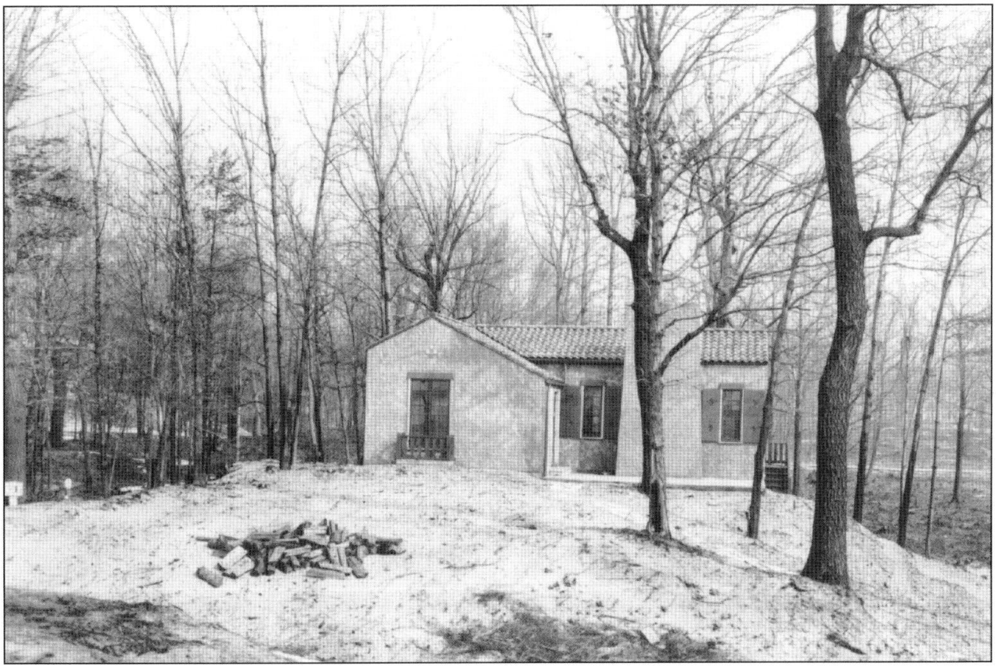

PLAN No. B2. Land investors sought to maximize their profits, and in this area industry was the most fruitful means of doing so. Consequently, South Chicago grew more dirty and congested while the north and west sides became the choice suburban areas. These conditions made South Chicago's residents extremely receptive to the lure of a resort development with convenient transportation links to their homes and factories. (Photo courtesy of Beverly Shores Museum and Art Gallery, Inc., Beverly Shores, Indiana.)

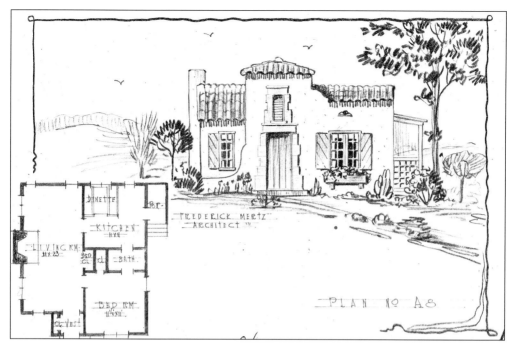

PLAN NO. A8. By the early 20th century, Chicago had the largest network of surface commuter railroads in the world, servicing an expanding urban area. This trolley and commuter rail system allowed increasing urban sprawl but dictated its direction of flow. Dense commercial and residential corridors spread along the trolley lines, with the more remote areas left to fill in more slowly. (Photo courtesy of Beverly Shores Museum and Art Gallery, Inc., Beverly Shores, Indiana.)

PLAN NO. E4. Urban trolleys were augmented by interurban railroad lines which boomed between the World Wars. These lines were usually serviced by high-speed, electrified, passenger cars between commuter stops which were generally more dispersed than the urban trollies. These lines offered frequent service directly from previously-remote rural towns to downtown Chicago, opening up the countryside as residential areas for downtown businessmen. Gradually, small interurban lines conglomerated into a few large railroads linking rural towns as far away as north central Illinois to Chicago. These lines often paralleled railroad passenger lines, but won most commuter passengers with more frequently scheduled runs. (Photo courtesy of Beverly Shores Museum and Art Gallery, Inc., Beverly Shores, Indiana.)

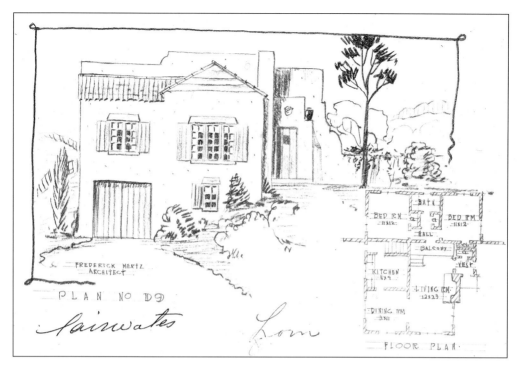

PLAN NO. D9. Unfortunately, Bartlett's first development push was foiled by the stock market crash of 1929 and the ensuing Depression. As stated earlier, only a small portion of the lots were built on, and the town site must have had the appearance of a ghost town. Some resort activity must have continued among clients wealthy enough to be unaffected by the Depression, but the original development plan was obviously not going to be realized.

LEO W. POST
CONSTRUCTION CO.
(Not Inc.)

Post Office Box No. 9
MICHIGAN CITY, IND.

Builders of Fine, Modern Residences

Dear Friend,

You can no   the
lowest prices in years.

By   ity
you can build a ne   e.

a question
Many good
marked
diti

We
of s   .
Please   t
your co   losed for

N CO

LAKE SHORE ADDITION, LEO W. POST CONSTRUCTION CO.

Four

SECOND
DEVELOPMENT PHASE
ROBERT BARTLETT ADMINISTRATION

BROADWAY, BEVERLY SHORES, 1930S. In 1933, Frederick Bartlett turned over control of Beverly shores to his brother Robert Bartlett in an effort to revive momentum. The Robert Bartlett Realty Company set about reviving interest in the community in spite of the Depression. Robert's efforts consisted of constructing public improvements, renewing the promotion of residential property, and organizing entertainment activities.

These new facilities were meant to house visitors drawn by such attractions as the new Theater of the Dunes, which Bartlett constructed at the intersection of Broadway and Beverly Drive. Through the summer it hosted drama teams from the Goodman Theater in Chicago performing current stage shows. (Photo courtesy of Beverly Shores Museum and Art Gallery, Inc., Beverly Shores, Indiana.)

BROADWAY, BEVERLY SHORES. The new realty company also upgraded Broadway and Lakefront Drive by lining them with double rows of poplar and elm trees, and by paving more streets to bring the total distance of paved roadway to 40 miles. The golf course was improved with the addition of underground sprinklers and enhanced maintenance.

Robert Bartlett's most significant accomplishment of 1933-34 was the renewal of residential construction. During this year, 16 new houses were constructed, almost doubling the previous number, and more than a million dollars of real estate was sold. Most of these houses were built from designs taken from the original plan book. Over the next few years, Leo Post of the Beverly Shores Construction Company constructed approximately 50 more Mediterranean Revival residences in the dunes. Robert capped off his success with the construction of his own $30,000 home, a large log lodge, on the top of a 112-foot dune overlooking the lake. His house was designed by an architect named Elmer William Marx, and was not at all rustic, boasting an elegant colonial interior and complete modern amenities. (Photo courtesy of Beverly Shores Museum and Art Gallery, Inc., Beverly Shores, Indiana.)

BEVERLY SHORES INN. Robert Bartlett's most significant accomplishment in spurring new growth was the construction of the Beverly Shores Inn in 1933. This hotel was constructed on the west side of Broadway a few hundred feet north of the Administration Building. This was a $100,000, two-story, fireproof building clad in sand-colored brick and executed in the Mediterranean Revival style. The hotel was U-shaped, with a one-story arcade sheltering the entrance in the front courtyard, and limestone emphasizing the string courses and entrances. As in earlier structures, the Spanish theme was emphasized on the exterior with arched windows in a central tower and a clay tile roof. However, the interior showed the influence of new styles in its use of Art Moderne furnishings, but still contained Spanish details such as stucco walls, cast iron chandeliers, and arched arcades between public rooms. The hotel boasted an elegant restaurant and bar, as well as a large dining room. (Photo courtesy of Beverly Shores Museum and Art Gallery, Inc., Beverly Shores, Indiana.)

GARDENS OF BEVERLY SHORES INN. A rear patio overlooked a formal Italian garden designed around a central pool and radiating paths. This garden contained unique pathways inlaid with mosaic tile fired by its designer, a Chicago artist named Mrs. Louis Van Hees Young, and it contained a rare collection of plants native to the dunes.

The developer's public works and the increased residential development also attracted private commercial investment to Beverly Shores. Even before the second development push, Joseph Greco had erected the town's first commercial structure to house his restaurant and inn in 1930. This was a two-story, stucco-clad structure ornamented with Spanish elements. The building burned in the mid-30s, but was replaced with the present restaurant building in 1946. (Photo courtesy of Beverly Shores Museum and Art Gallery, Inc., Beverly Shores, Indiana.)

GARDENS OF BEVERLY SHORES INN. Robert Bartlett's vigor in promoting his brother's resort resulted in a relative building boom of commercial structures in the mid-1930s. Ignas Lenard had a beach stand erected just west of the town public beach, but soon expanded it into the Lenard Casino. Leo Post constructed the Casino of white terra-cotta panels with streamlined string courses of colored terra cotta. This facade encased a two-story rectangular building with a flat roof. This seems to be one of the few buildings erected in Beverly Shores in the 1930s which was not Spanish in character, but it was later expanded and remodeled to blend more inconspicuously with the town's Spanish tradition. (Photo courtesy of Beverly Shores Museum and Art Gallery, Inc., Beverly Shores, Indiana.)

Post Office. A post office building was erected on Broadway at its intersection with Beverly Drive in 1935. This was a two-story commercial structure of cream brick with a Spanish tile roof projecting beyond the center of its parapet. This structure was destroyed after the area became a National Park in the 1970s.

A Deli and Grocery store was erected at Broadway and Atwater, joining the restaurant, theater, and post office in a small commercial district. (Photo courtesy of Beverly Shores Museum and Art Gallery, Inc., Beverly Shores, Indiana.)

FIRE STATION. The maintenance crews for the resort used their first permanent garage just south of the hotel on the opposite side of Broadway during 1933-34. This building was a one-story brick structure built of similar materials to the hotel, with two front garage doors and an office area. Both the hotel and the garage, later used as the fire station, burned down in the 1970s. (Photo courtesy of Beverly Shores Museum and Art Gallery, Inc., Beverly Shores, Indiana.)

RETAIL BUILDING SUPPLY STORE AND YARD. Most of this construction was carried out by Leo Post's Beverly Shores Construction Company, causing the company to expand and prosper. In about 1935, the company constructed a headquarters building, a retail building supply yard, and hardware store on its own railroad spur just south of the Administration Building. This two-story building was similar to the Casino in its use of terra cotta cladding and ornamental banding. It was serviced by lumber sheds and storage facilities on its back lot. (Photos courtesy of Beverly Shores Museum and Art Gallery, Inc., Beverly Shores, Indiana.)

SCHOOL AND GAS STATION. The elementary school was erected on Bellview Avenue within a few years after the development of Beverly Shores began. A major addition to the school was made in the 1960s, however the building has since been destroyed.

The service station was built by Leo Post's Beverly Shores Construction Co. and was owned and operated by Jack and Jewel Widmar for many years. (Photos courtesy of Beverly Shores Museum and Art Gallery, Inc., Beverly Shores, Indiana.)

ROBERT BARTLETT BEVERLY SHORES HOME. Robert Bartlett's $30,000 log cabin residence was completed in time for anniversary week. This was a 9-room home atop a 112-foot dune, affording a view of 3 states. Floors and wall panelings were reproductions of those in colonial homes of the late-17th and mid-18th centuries. The furniture was Early American in design. (Photo courtesy of Beverly Shores Museum and Art Gallery, Inc., Beverly Shores, Indiana.)

LENARD'S CASINO RESTAURANT. During the 1930s, a steady trickle of homes gave Beverly Shores a more settled look. Mr. and Mrs. Joseph Greco erected the first commercial structure to house their restaurant, Casa Del Lago, in 1930. It burnt down in the mid-1930s and the owners replaced it with the present building which Mr. and Mrs. Joseph Greco II began operating in 1946. In 1934, Bartlett built a beach stand and restaurant for Mr. and Mrs. Ignas Lenard which they expanded into Lenard's Casino. New owners purchased the hotel-restaurant in 1965 and transformed it into the Red Lantern Inn. (Photo courtesy of Indiana Dunes National Lakeshore, Porter, Indiana.)

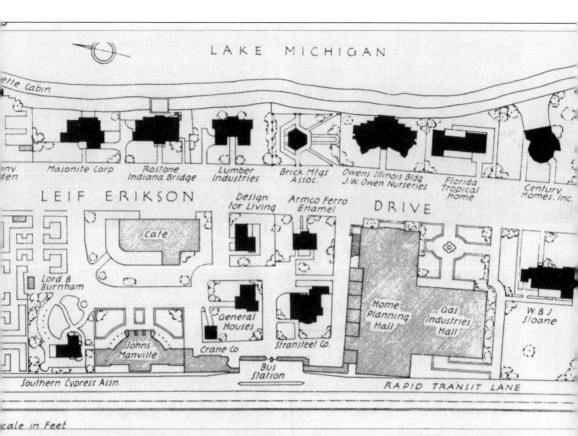

LAKE MICHIGAN

ette Cabin

Masonite Corp   Rostone   Lumber   Brick Mfgs   Owens·Illinois Bldg   Florida   Century
any   Indiana Bridge Industries   Assoc.   J.W. Owen Nurseries   Tropical   Homes. Inc.
den   Home

LEIF ERIKSON   Design   Armco Ferro   DRIVE
                        for Living   Enamel

Cafe

Lord &   W. & J.
Burnham   Home   Gas   Sloane
                                                Planning Industries
                        General   Hall   Hall
                        Houses

                        Crane Co.   Stransteel Co.
Johns·
Manville   Bus
                                  Station
Southern Cypress Assn.   RAPID TRANSIT LANE

cale in Feet

HOME AND INDUSTRIAL ARTS GROUP EXHIBITION AREA AT CENTURY OF PROGRESS. All of these physical improvements were accompanied and promoted by a colorful publicity campaign in the Chicago media. Everything from newspaper ads to society-style sections made mention of the beautiful and convenient resort of Beverly Shores. However, in 1935 Robert Bartlett devised his most enduring publicity stunt, buying a piece of the 1933-34 Chicago World's Fair. The 1933-34 "Century of Progress" Chicago World's Fair was an extremely popular event, even though it did not have the far-reaching cultural impact of the 1893 Fair. This fair overcame extremely depressed economic conditions and drew more than 38 million visitors during an unprecedented two years of operation while earning a substantial profit. The Century of Progress was planned to highlight the technical advances of modern society while displaying a traditional selection of cultural exhibits from around the world. Critics argue that its designers used modern-looking, stage-set gimmicks to attract a wide audience to an exhibition complex executed in an essentially traditional manner. All of the principle architects and planners for the major exhibition areas were formalists trained in the Beaux Arts tradition. (Photo courtesy of Beverly Shores Museum and Art Gallery, Inc., Beverly Shores, Indiana.)

THE MOST VISITED — THE MOST

HOME AND INDUSTRIAL ART GROUP DISPLAY HOMES. The technological emphasis of the fair did pioneer new directions in everyday home technology. Along with exhibiting the latest in automobiles, radios, washing machines, and toasters, fair planners organized a group primarily composed of building material manufacturers to construct a series of model homes exhibiting how their materials could be innovatively combined to create modern houses. The resulting conglomeration of buildings was called the Home and Industrial Arts Exhibit, and was prominently located adjacent to the grand central court. This exhibition contained the following houses designed by their respective architects: the House of Tomorrow by George Fred Keck; the Rostone House by Walter Scholer; the Armco-Ferro House by Robert Smith Jr.; the Stran-Steel House by O'Dell and Rowland; the Model Farm House by Holsman and Holsman; (Photo courtesy of Beverly Shores Museum and Art Gallery, Inc., Beverly Shores, Indiana.)

OST T _KED-OF — HOMES IN THE WORLD

the Brick House by Andrew Rebori; the American Forest Products Industries House by Ernest Grunsfield; the Glass Block Building for the Owens-Illinois Glass Company; the Design for Living House by John C.B. Moore; the Masonite House by Frazier and Raftery; the Florida Tropical House by Robert Law Weed; and the Cypress Log House by Hetherington Architects. This housing exhibit was enormously successful and it received widespread favorable coverage in the general national media, even though the architectural journals criticized many of the designs as crude. The House of Tomorrow, with its extensive use of glass curtain walls, was a particularly popular subject for journalists. (Photo courtesy of Beverly Shores Museum and Art Gallery, Inc., Beverly Shores, Indiana.)

ROSTONE HOUSE ON A BARGE. Documentation shows that Bartlett hired Civil Engineers, Ltd. of Chicago to devise a means of relocating four of the buildings, which were too heavy to move by truck from the Fair to Beverly Shores, intact. This company loaded the buildings onto barges at the Fair site, then towed the barges across the southern tip of Lake Michigan to Beverly Shores in the spring of 1935. Upon reaching the shore, they were rolled upon telephone poles onto a temporary pier of stacked logs. This pier was constructed with several levels stepping up to Lakefront Drive where the houses were to be placed. Using only men and mules for power, the houses were jacked up to each succeeding level and rolled closer to their new foundations. (Photo courtesy of Beverly Shores Museum and Art Gallery, Inc., Beverly Shores, Indiana.)

ARMCO-FERRO HOUSE ON THE PIER. (Photo courtesy of Beverly Shores Museum and Art Gallery, Inc., Beverly Shores, Indiana.)

HOUSE OF TOMORROW, 1934, AT THE FAIR. This House of Tomorrow was probably the most architecturally and technologically interesting of the houses in the Home and Industrial Arts Exhibit, and is certainly the most interesting of those moved to Beverly Shores. George Fred Keck, a young Chicago architect at the beginning of an outstanding career, designed this house of materials previously used in industrial applications. Its basic structure is similar in concept to Frank Lloyd Wright's tree-like skyscrapers. A broad central steel cylinder support formed the tree trunk, and supported two levels of 12 radiating steel joists which supported its two progressively-smaller upper floors and a crowning roof. The cylinder-support contained the utilities (electric, heat and cooling runs, waste lines, etc..) serving the structure.

The floor joists framed pie-shaped wedges of concrete flooring as well as a finish surface of tile or wood. The branching floor joists ended at light posts which bore a portion of the floor load. The outside edges of the floor structure framed the large single panes of commercial plate glass which abutted one another and formed a continuous ring of exterior walls and fenestration for each level. The roof was made of compressed asphalt boards which formed terraces as each level stepped back. (Photo courtesy of Beverly Shores Museum and Art Gallery, Inc., Beverly Shores, Indiana.)

HOUSE OF TOMORROW, 1934, AT THE FAIR. This building was an interesting blend of technological showmanship and the influences of European Modernism. It embodied the "machine for living" ideas of Corbusier in its use of simple geometries and its closed glass box environment of sealed windows and completely mechanical climate control. However, its odd exterior shape, its inclusion of an airplane hangar in the first floor, and its expensive yet gimmicky interior appliances all display its roots as a manufacturer's showcase. The House of Tomorrow was not an inexpensive structure, it cost between $20–$25,000 to build, and it was projected to have a life span of 50 years.

The House of Tomorrow's nationwide publicity made it an extremely attractive promotional addition to Beverly Shores from Robert Bartlett's perspective. He must have placed particular value on this house since it was one of the structures on which he spent the additional cost of moving it by barge. Bartlett had the house sited high on a dune overlooking the lake to take advantage of its transparent walls. (Photos courtesy of Beverly Shores Museum and Art Gallery, Inc., Beverly Shores, Indiana.)

ARMCO-FERRO HOUSE, 1934, AT THE FAIR. This house was much more of a production-model structure than was typical of houses in the Exhibit. It was produced by a steel firm located near Cleveland, the American Rolling Mill Company, and the Ferro Enamel Corporation, to display the new "frameless" steel method of construction which they had developed in the previous years.

This house was a relatively small two-story rectangular structure, with somewhat conventional proportions and design elements. It had an informal interior plan which included a garage and a rooftop sunroom. Its most emphasized trait at the Fair was not its stylistic design but its safety and low maintenance due to its steel construction.

The structure of this house was fabricated entirely of pre-cut steel welded together at the construction site. A steel chassis replaced the traditional foundation sill, and served as a base to which corrugated sections of steel were mounted. These corrugated sections were faced on the exterior with enameled steel panels backed with a liner of stainless steel, and on the interior with gypsum board, thus forming 2 by 6-inch air cavities. The flat roof was constructed in a similar manner.

The Armco-Ferro House must have been one of the easier houses to move among those barged across the lake. It was the first to be landed and was moved the farthest from the landing site. (Photo courtesy of Beverly Shores Museum and Art Gallery, Inc., Beverly Shores, Indiana.)

ROSTONE HOUSE, 1934, AT THE FAIR. Rostone, Inc. of Lafayette, Indiana, and the Indiana Bridge Company constructed the Rostone House as a showpiece of their new product. Rostone was a synthetic building stone formed from limestone waste and shale, then shaped into panel sizes required for specific buildings. This was a smooth material resembling sandstone but much easier to install because of its factory-formed sizes and its use of cast-in fastening devices. The Rostone panels were bolted directly to a steel frame using bolts threaded through steel and into nuts precast into the panels, both interior and exterior.

It was logical that this Indiana partnership would choose the prominent Hoosier Architect Walter Scholer to design their show house. He created a rather monumental geometric composition of forms which fit in with the general architectural theme of the Fair, yet showed no dominating stylistic traits. The house was basically rectangular in form with a raised and projecting center bay containing the entrance. It had an informal interior plan oriented toward large windows on the back of the house. The front wall was a largely unpierced monolithic facade backed by service rooms and a garage. Shallow relief carvings surrounded the entrance and possibly other key areas.

Bartlett sited this house, which must have been quite heavy, directly between the beach and Lakefront Drive. This location was ideal since its blank face was oriented toward the road and its expansive windows toward the lake. For many years, the Clifton Utley family, a Chicago newsman and broadcaster, used this as a summer home. (Photo courtesy of Beverly Shores Museum and Art Gallery, Inc., Beverly Shores, Indiana.)

CYPRESS HOUSE, 1934, AT THE FAIR. This house was designed by Murray Hetherington, a Chicago architect, for the Southern Cypress Growers Association as a demonstration of the versatility and durability of this unusual wood. It was constructed as a rather small rustic cabin of frame construction sheathed in pecky cypress log siding. Its wide overhanging eaves were ornamented with cypress knees resembling grotesque animal heads, and its roof was sheathed in cypress shakes. The interior was dominated by a great room with a limestone fireplace. When exhibited at the Fair, this building was surrounded by a rustic landscape of ponds, cedar bridges, and another cabin joined to the main structure by a pergola-sheltered walkway. After relocation to Beverly Shores, it was sited on the front face of a dune overlooking Lake Michigan, directly east of the House of Tomorrow. (Photo courtesy of Beverly Shores Museum and Art Gallery, Inc., Beverly Shores, Indiana.)

Preparing for New Foundation, Next to Cypress House at Beverly Shores. The Country Home Model Farmhouse was designed by Holsman and Holsman Architects of Chicago as an example of how innovative materials and forms could create an unconventional farmhouse which was efficient and inexpensive. Its construction was sponsored by *Country Home Magazine*. This house represented a radical break with traditional farmhouses by utilizing a two-story, pyramidal-roof, brick structure housing a casual interior plan designed around a large living/dining room.

The most innovative aspect of this farmhouse was its means of construction. This was the first house in the U.S. to be constructed of tilt-up reinforced brick panels. These panels were formed by laying bricks in geometric patterns within the square gaps of a grid of reinforcing bars, all inside a wooden form. Grout was poured into the joints between bricks and the whole panel was tipped up and bolted in place when dry. The second-level floor was formed by pouring concrete into unique "I-pans." The interior wall and roof were also built using these heavy construction techniques. One unusual amenity created by this type of construction was a large sun deck on the roof of the attached garage.

This house was isolated from the other Home and Industrial Arts homes moved to Beverly Shores. It was sited on the west side of Broadway, just north of Beverly Drive on Jones Street. (Photo courtesy of Beverly Shores Museum and Art Gallery, Inc., Beverly Shores, Indiana.)

FLORIDA HOUSE, 1934, AT THE FAIR. The Florida House is one of the most interesting of the Home and Industrial Arts Exhibit's structures. It was designed by prominent Miami architect Robert Law Weed (designer of the University of Miami and one of the first modernists in the South), for the State of Florida as an example of how such an unusual climate could dictate home design.

Because South Florida does not endure the freeze-thaw cycle so damaging to masonry buildings in the North, Weed chose to build a structure which was essentially a single masonry mass made up of reinforced concrete, concrete block, hollow clay tile, and stucco on a concrete slab. These thick walls cooled the house while supporting concrete beams and a flat-roof terrace. The windows were steel casements sheltered by a wide projecting awning of concrete integrated into the structure of the house. This was meant to shelter the windows from sun or rain, while allowing in the lower rays of the winter sun. This was an elegant house, accented by Spanish ceramic tile on the interior, but without the historical Spanish references common in Florida resorts up to that time. Instead, such modern elements as porthole windows, cantilevered roofs, and aluminum railings characterized the house. The playful resort feel of the house was highlighted by bright pink exterior paint. (Photos courtesy of Beverly Shores Museum and Art Gallery, Inc., Beverly Shores, Indiana.)

COLONIAL VILLAGE AT THE WORLD'S FAIR, 1934. One of the less-publicized cultural attractions of the fair was its Colonial Village, located at the far eastern edge of the grounds, far from the grand court. This exhibit capitalized on the contemporary popularity of colonial culture and specifically its architecture. The Colonial Village attempted to capture the charm of such attractions as Colonial Williamsburg by assembling replicas of the country's most famous colonial structures at reduced scale. Tallmadge and Watson of Chicago were the architects of the exhibit but it consisted of rather inaccurate replicas ranging from churches to blacksmiths' shops. The Village contained Old North Church, Independence Hall, Mount Vernon, a Virginia Tavern, the House of Seven Gables, the Wayside Inn, the Massachusetts Governor's House, Wakefield Manor, Paul Revere's House, Ben Franklin's House, the Betsy Ross House, and the Village Smithy. (Photo courtesy of Beverly Shores Museum and Art Gallery, Inc., Beverly Shores, Indiana.)

	Purchase Price	Moving Cost
Mount Vernon	$1,000.00	$2,500.00
Virginia Tavern	500.00	2,300.00
Wayside Inn	600.00	1,900.00
Paul Revere House	500.00	1,900.00
House of 7 Gables	700.00	1,900.00
Ben Franklin House	500.00	1,800.00
Village Smithy	300.00	950.00
Including hauling stone fireplace and taking same down.		
Wakefield	600.00	1,400.00
Governor's Mansion	700.00	2,000.00
Old North Church	600.00	2,100.00
	Total $6,000.00	Total $18,750.00

COLONIAL VILLAGE STRUCTURES MOVED FROM FAIR TO BEVERLY SHORES. When the fair closed on Halloween night, 1934, its managing company was left with the daunting task of returning its site to park land within the year required by their contract with the city. The company was forced to offer its structures for sale at a fraction of their initial cost through advertisements in Chicago newspapers. Most of the larger structures were dismantled and sold for their parts or as scrap, but the smaller buildings offered buyers the chance to move them and re-use them as residences and small commercial establishments.

Robert Bartlett saw these surplus Fair structures as an ideal means of promoting Beverly Shores while enlarging his building stock at a reasonable cost. He purchased structures from both the Home and Industrial Arts Exhibit and the Colonial Village and moved them to Beverly Shores in the most cost-efficient manner available for each particular building. (Photo courtesy of Beverly Shores Museum and Art Gallery, Inc., Beverly Shores, Indiana.)

MOUNT VERNON, BEVERLY SHORES. The Colonial Village exhibit was an interesting contrast to the Fair's overall modernistic theme, and it reveals how most Americans still held a strong fascination for our romanticized colonial history.

Bartlett's largest purchase was from the Colonial Village exhibit. These structures were all of frame construction but were originally sheathed with either grooved wood siding to simulate clapboards, or with scored gypsum board to simulate brick. Their roofs were of random width and colored composition shingles over wood decking. The only finished areas in these structures were their first levels, which had board floors. The buildings contained little plumbing and no heating fixtures. (Photo courtesy of Indiana Dunes National Lakeshore, Porter, Indiana.)

LONGFELLOW'S WAYSIDE INN, BEVERLY SHORES. (Photo courtesy of Indiana Dunes National Lakeshore, Porter, Indiana.)

THE OLD NORTH CHURCH, BEVERLY SHORES. The lightweight nature of the Colonial Village structures made them easy to transport. In the spring of 1935, Bartlett had the buildings dismantled and loaded onto trucks for shipment to his resort. They were then re-erected, plumbed, and wired for habitation, and then sold to private buyers. Bartlett placed most of these buildings in the southern area of the town near and along Broadway to add interest and density to this flat area behind the dunes which had yet to attract residential development. (Photos courtesy of Indiana Dunes National Lakeshore, Porter, Indiana)

VIRGINIA TAVERN, BEVERLY SHORES. (Photo courtesy of Indiana Dunes National Lakeshore, Porter, Indiana)

BEN FRANKLIN HOUSE, BEVERLY SHORES. Joseph Bentlas, president of B.W. Construction Company, was the originator and owner of the Colonial Village World Fair attraction. It occupied a 2-acre site on "Main Street" in 1934, which was the 1933 Midway. It was an investment of $225,000. It occupied the former sites of several Midway attractions, among them the Battle of Gettysburg, Miss America, the Life Show, the Funnies, Aero Whirlplane, the Freak Show, and others. Benjamin H. Marshall, Chicago architect, was the general manager of the Colonial Village. The staff wore colonial costumes and wherever concessions were allowed, the materials sold were authentic reproductions of something colonial. (Photo courtesy of Indiana Dunes National Lakeshore, Porter, Indiana.)

HOUSE OF PAUL REVERE, BEVERLY SHORES. (Photo courtesy of Indiana Dunes National Lakeshore, Porter, Indiana)

STREAMLINED MODERN METAL HOUSE. A Chicago firm, Estate Homes, Inc., announced in the spring of 1936 the selection of 49 sites in Beverly Shores for its ultra-modern metal homes. John A. Stearns, president, advised that Walter W. Ahlschlager will be developing the sites. Ahlschlager's basic patents cover the prefabrication and construction of a type of all-metal dwelling, to be erected in Beverly Shores. The architect, Ahlschlager, stated the homes to be built will be of 99.6 per cent pure zinc plates. The first unit, a five-room building, costing $4,250, was placed on Stillwater Avenue, west of Broadway. (Photos courtesy of Beverly Shores Museum and Art Gallery, Inc., Beverly Shores, Indiana)

LUSTRON HOME. Erected in 1949, this Lustron, all-steel, porcelain-enameled, prefabricated house was handled by dealer-builder Tonn & Blank of Michigan City, Indiana. Three other Lustron homes were erected on Lake Front Drive and State Park Road. These houses featured built-in steel furniture, interior steel sliding pocket doors, radiant ceiling heating, and a combination clothes washer and dishwasher. (Photo courtesy of Beverly Shores Museum and Art Gallery, Inc., Beverly Shores, Indiana.)

INTERNATIONAL STYLE HOME. Built in 1949 on Lake Front Drive, this International Style architecture, applied to a seasonal dwelling, was designed by Swiss architect Otto Kolb. He was influenced by the architectural concepts of the Bauhaus School of Germany of the early 1930s. It received European acclaim from their press and magazines. The house was placed on the National Registry of Historic Places by the United States Department of the Interior. (Photo courtesy of Beverly Shores Museum and Art Gallery, Inc., Beverly Shores, Indiana.)

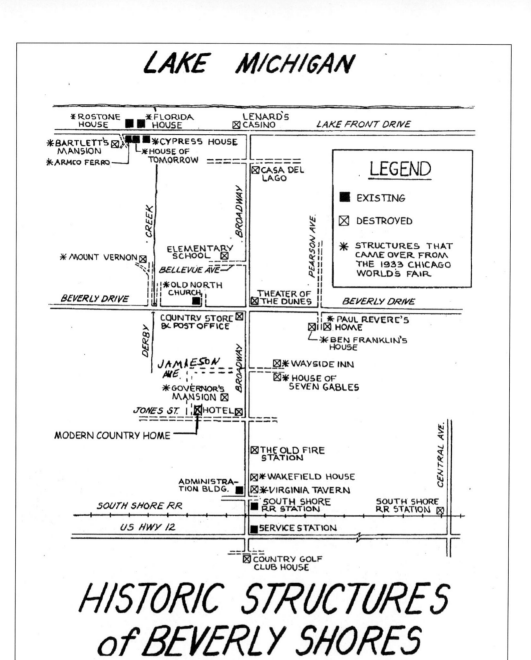

HISTORIC STRUCTURES of BEVERLY SHORES

Map labels:

LAKE MICHIGAN

LAKE FRONT DRIVE

* ROSTONE HOUSE
* FLORIDA HOUSE
LENARD'S CASINO

* BARTLETT'S MANSION
* CYPRESS HOUSE
* HOUSE OF TOMORROW
* ARMCO FERRO

CASA DEL LAGO

LEGEND
■ EXISTING
⊠ DESTROYED
* STRUCTURES THAT CAME OVER FROM THE 1933 CHICAGO WORLD'S FAIR

CREEK

BROADWAY

PEARSON AVE.

* MOUNT VERNON
ELEMENTARY SCHOOL
BELLEVUE AVE.

* OLD NORTH CHURCH

BEVERLY DRIVE

THEATER OF THE DUNES

BEVERLY DRIVE

DERBY

COUNTRY STORE & POST OFFICE

* PAUL REVERE'S HOME
* BEN FRANKLIN'S HOUSE

JAMIESON AVE.

BROADWAY

* WAYSIDE INN
* HOUSE OF SEVEN GABLES

* GOVERNOR'S MANSION

JONES ST. HOTEL

MODERN COUNTRY HOME

CENTRAL AVE.

THE OLD FIRE STATION

* WAKEFIELD HOUSE

ADMINISTRATION BLDG.

* VIRGINIA TAVERN

SOUTH SHORE RR

SOUTH SHORE RR STATION

SOUTH SHORE RR STATION

US HWY 12

SERVICE STATION

COUNTRY GOLF CLUB HOUSE

HISTORIC STRUCTURES OF BEVERLY SHORES. The addition of the World's Fair houses, as well as the other improvements introduced under the younger Bartlett, gave Beverly Shores a sufficiently strong image to continue to attract visitors and residents throughout the decade before World War II. The town maintained its status as a popular resort for affluent South Chicagoans, while those of more modest means made short weekend trips to neighboring Indiana Dunes State Park. A new group of residents attracted to the resort in the 1930s was made up of professors and residents from the University of Chicago and Hyde Park area. For these teachers, Beverly Shores was only a quick interurban trip from campus to the secluded resort. (Photo courtesy of Beverly Shores Museum and Art Gallery, Inc., Beverly Shores, Indiana.)

...*Off to a good start at*
BEVERLY SHORES

○ TO ACCOMMODATE the increasing number of golfers, bathers, hikers and other outdoor folk who come to Beverly Shores for rest and recreation, a new, thoroughly modern hotel has been built on Broadway, opposite the South Shore Line station. Here you are assured of metropolitan hotel comforts and conveniences in the heart of duneland beauty. The hostelry has large, light, and airy guest rooms equipped with modern all-steel furniture. Excellent food, from a sandwich to a full course dinner, is obtainable in the hotel's dining-room, at prices no higher than those asked in less pleasant surroundings.

Beverly Shores hotel is strategically located, close to the golf course and within walking distance of the beach. The 18-hole golf course, hailed by professionals as one of the three foremost courses in America, is the scene of historic playing by such stars as Sarazen, Cooper, Armour, McDonald, Dawson, Murray, and many others who have participated in the hotly contested tournaments staged here.

Here are two sets of tees—one for championship meets and one for regular play. The course offers you golf at its best—3362 yards going out, 3209 coming in. Par is 36-35, total 71. The fairway watering systems assures green fairways throughout the season. From the clubhouse veranda you can enjoy an excellent view of Lake Michigan. The clubhouse is of Spanish architecture, with a commodious lounge, dining-room, lockers, and showers. Adjoining it is an outdoor dancing pavilion.

Now that the nearby hotel is completed, early-birds can bring their golf clubs on the eve of play, sleep

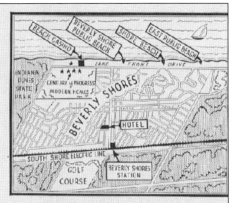

soundly at the new hostelry, and be awakened before sunrise so that they can step over to the course and start play in the light of earliest dawn. Golf in the dunes is a rare experience such as is enjoyed only at the famous seaside courses of England and Scotland, and America's east and west coasts where similar natural conditions prevail. Beverly Shores offers the only golf of this kind in the entire metropolitan Chicago area.

Within view of the course, and adjoining the hotel, is the Beverly Shores Botanical Garden with its wide variety of flora natural to the Dunes region. Here arctic and tropical plants can be found growing within a few yards of each other—one of the few places in the world where such rare combinations are to be seen in their natural environment.

Chicago, South Shore & South Bend Railroad
140 SOUTH DEARBORN, CHICAGO

Hourly service from downtown Chicago direct to Beverly Shores station on fast, comfortable South Shore Line trains provides the most convenient method of transportation. Five convenient stations at Randolph St., Van Buren St., Roosevelt Road, 53rd Street (Hyde Park) and 63rd Street (Woodlawn) make this means of transportation more accessible. For information telephone State 0517, or write Traffic Department, C. S. S. & S. B. R. R., Room 908, 140 S. Dearborn, Chicago.

SOUTH SHORE LINE PROMOTIONAL BROCHURE OF BEVERLY SHORES. (Photos courtesy of Calumet Regional Archives of Indiana University Northwest, Gary, Indiana.)

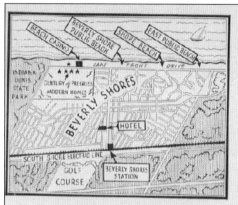

Thrill to the cool blue waters at
BEVERLY SHORES

◐ COOL, blue Lake Michigan, vast swimming pool for Chicagoland's millions, boasts many miles of beaches, most attractive of which are those of the Dunes. Here clean, smooth sands, sloping down from verdant hills into the clear waters of the lake, make for ideal bathing conditions. Swimming and sun-bathing here are pleasures long to be remembered.

Increasing beach attendance on the dunes lakefront, especially at Beverly Shores beach, has made it necessary to provide accommodations for visitors. Consequently, there has been added to the general improvement program of Beverly Shores a new $40,000 beach-casino project. It includes a 50- by 250-foot riparian rights location just west of the Broadway public beach; and a modern casino building. As seen from the lake, this structure is three stories high, having a beach level, a street level, and a top, third-story level. On the beach level, the interior was designed for lockers, showers, and a supply department of equipment for swimming, sun-bathing and other aquatic sports. Above this, on the second floor with its entrance level with the street, arrangements are planned for dining and dancing. Here you will find seaside atmosphere and surroundings similar to those enjoyed in other fashionable waterfronts of the world—the Riviera, Deauville, the Lido, Scheveningen, Atlantic City and Palm Beach.

Now it will be possible for people of the middle-west to experience seashore delights close to home. Whether you want an hour's swim or several weeks' vacation, all you need   step aboard a South Shore Electric Line train   be whisked

with speed—and in comfort—to beautiful Beverly Shores. Here you can enjoy golf at its best; a refreshing dip in Lake Michigan; pleasant hikes over winding trails through the rolling, wooded hills where lake breezes play; courteous modern hotel service and facilities; dining and dancing at a new beach casino right at the water's edge; and free inspection of the famous "Century of Progress" exhibit homes which have been selected for permanent location at Beverly Shores.

Plan now to see the many new attractions enhancing the natural beauty and charm of the Beverly Shores section of the world famous Indiana Dunes.

Hourly service from downtown Chicago direct to Beverly Shores station on fast, comfortable South Shore Line trains, provides the most convenient method of transportation. Five convenient stations at Randolph St., Van Buren St., Roosevelt Road, 53rd St. (Hyde Park) and 63rd St. (Woodlawn) make this means of transportation more accessible. For information telephone State 0517, or write Traffic Department, C. S. S. & S. B. R. R., Room 908, 140 S. Dearborn, Chicago.

SOUTH SHORE LINE PROMOTIONAL BROCHURE OF BEVERLY SHORES. (Photos courtesy of Calumet Regional Archives of Indiana University Northwest, Gary, Indiana.)

Five

BEVERLY SHORES:
THIRD PHASE

TOWN STATUS—SAVE THE DUNES COUNCIL—
INDIANA DUNES NATIONAL LAKESHORE PARK

BEVERLY SHORES FIRST TOWN COUNCIL. Pictured, from left to right, are Carl Gasteyer, William Mork, Floyd Williams, Leo Post, Earl Braginton, and John Consdorf. The Second World War brought an end to this rather exclusive chapter of Beverly Shores' history. Bartlett had closed the hotel, clubhouse, and golf course and began phasing out his other areas of interest. By this time all of Bartlett's original lots had been sold to investors and there was little reason to remain active in the maintenance of the resort. In 1946, Robert Bartlett turned over all of his remaining holdings, including the rights of way, the public beach, the administration building, and all maintenance facilities, to the local landowners. In 1947, Beverly Shores was incorporated as an autonomous town. (Photo courtesy of Beverly Shores Museum and Art Gallery, Inc., Beverly Shores, Indiana.)

DEPARTMENT OF COMMERCE
WILLIAM C. FOSTER, Acting Secretary

BUREAU OF THE CENSUS
J. C. CAPT, Director

I nd - cities + Towns, 138-BE

CURRENT POPULATION REPORTS

SPECIAL CENSUSES

| May 5, 1948 | ~ Washington 25, D. C. | Series P-28, No. 302 |

SPECIAL CENSUS OF BEVERLY SHORES, INDIANA: MARCH 15, 1948

The total population of the town of Beverly Shores, Porter County, Indiana, on March 15, 1948, was 484, according to the final results of a special census announced today by J. C. Capt, Director, Bureau of the Census, Department of Commerce. The population was predominantly white. There were 239 males and 245 females (including 1 nonwhite female). Beverly Shores was incorporated as a town on January 2, 1947.

The number of occupied dwelling units in Beverly Shores was 144 on March 15, 1948. The population per occupied dwelling unit was 3.36.

BEVERLY SHORES CENSUSES REPORT. The town's growth was restricted by its lack of a municipal sewer or water system, which reduced the density of new homes. This major infrastructure had not been needed in order for Bartlett to market vacant lots. The scattered residents did not form a large enough tax base to bear the enormous cost for the installation of a public water or sewer system. Consequently, Beverly Shores' post-war growth was limited to a relatively small number of new residences, as well as a slow transition from a purely resort community to one with an equal number of permanent residents.

Industry's gradual destruction of natural areas along the Indiana Lakeshore throughout the first half of the 1900s caused increasing concern among environmentalists. A movement to turn Beverly Shores into a National Lakeshore Park grew rapidly after World War II, eventually resulting in the Federal acquisition of two-thirds of the original town of Beverly Shores in 1966. Although much of the acquired land was marsh or wooded areas which had not been heavily developed, it effectively ended any chance of realizing the resort as originally planned. (Photo courtesy of Beverly Shores Museum and Art Gallery, Inc., Beverly Shores, Indiana.)

SAVE-THE-DUNES COUNCIL PRESIDENT AND FOUNDER, DOROTHY BUELL. The Save-the-Dunes Council was established in 1952 to preserve the remaining unspoiled Dunes areas from destruction, spurred by fears that heavy industry and electric generating stations would destroy them. Initially, the Council hoped to buy the dunes between Ogden Dunes and Dune Acres with funds raised from private sources. These efforts proved insufficient. Next, Council founder Dorothy Buell approached the state of Indiana to extend the Indiana Dunes State Park. This in turn proved fruitless because Indiana state government wanted the area for a proposed deep-water port and industrial development. Appeals to Indiana's two U.S. Senators to help preserve the Dunes through federal action fell on deaf ears. So the Council turned to U.S. Senator Paul Douglas of Illinois. (Photo courtesy of Save-the-Dunes Council, Michigan City, Indiana.)

AN AWARD TO DOROTHY BUELL IN THE CAUSE OF CONSERVATION. (Photo courtesy of Save-the-Dunes Council, Michigan City, Indiana.)

HOLLIN' HILL, 1960, DESTROYED FOR PORT OF INDIANA. For two decades, the Great Depression and World War II and its aftermath pushed the issue of saving any more dune land into the background. These two momentous events, however, did nothing to halt the progression of industrial and commercial development in the dunes. As a result of Indiana Dunes State Park's enormous popularity, Frederick Bartlett Realty Company developed a large tract on the park's east boundary into a resort community called Beverly Shores. A component of the realtor's promotion was the 1935 acquisition and relocation of six model homes from Chicago's 1933-34 "Century of Progress" Exposition, as well as other structures modeled after famous American Colonial buildings. Pleased by the wide appeal and revenues generated by the Dunes State Park, the State of Indiana did not seek to expand or make any substantial developments to it. Rather, the state began exploring ways to induce more industry into its sliver of lakeshore. (Photos courtesy of Save-the-Dunes Council, Michigan City, Indiana.)

BETHLEHEM STEEL PROPERTY BEFORE CONSTRUCTION OF STEEL PLANT. In 1949, and Ogden Dunes family visited White Sands National Monument. Dorothy Richardson Buell, while moved by White Sands' grandeur, thought her own Indiana Dunes possessed greater qualities. As a young girl, Buell had performed in the Prairie Club-sponsored dunes pageants. Returning home, the Buells stopped for dinner in Gary where Dorothy Buell spotted a fateful sign announcing the formation of a citizens' group to save the dunes. Led by a University of Chicago professor, the Indiana Dunes Preservation Council (IDPC) identified unspoiled areas and recommended nearly seven miles of lakeshore for preservation. The IDPC garnered few positive developments. (Photos courtesy of Save-the-Dunes Council, Michigan City, Indiana.)

SANDMINING—DESTROYING THE DUNES. In early 1952, during a meeting of the Chicago Conservation Council, Dorothy Buell advised that historical precedent be followed to reignite the dunes preservation movement. Buell recounted Bess Sheehan's struggle and recommended that the effort be heralded by women. After the meeting, Buell decided to follow Sheehan's example and lead the revived movement herself.

On June 20, 1952, 21 women congregated in the Buell home and listened to Bess Sheehan relate events of 30 years past. The group discussed an alarming 1949 Corps of Engineers report which advocated a deep-water port for Indiana. While not opposed to the port, the group called for adding nearly 5 miles of lakeshore to the Dunes State park. The women announced to journalists they would dedicate their lives to saving the dunes. With that assertion, the Save-the-Dunes Council was born. (Photos courtesy of Save-the-Dunes Council, Michigan City, Indiana.)

CAMPING, 1960, ON BETHLEHEM STEEL LAND BY THE DUSTIN FAMILY. Indiana's opposition to adding more land to the Dunes State Park soon became apparent to the Save-the-Dunes Council. A united front of the political and business communities sought to maximize economic development along the limited lakeshore. The idea of setting aside more parkland was anathema to the economic planners who were working to secure Federal funds to construct a gigantic "Port of Indiana" at Burns Harbor (or Ditch). Expanding the existing mills and attracting still other steel companies to the area were other top priorities. (Photos courtesy of Save-The-Dunes Council, Michigan City, Indiana)

BETHLEHEM STEEL PROPERTY BEFORE CONSTRUCTION, 1959. (Photos courtesy of Save-The-Dunes Council, Michigan City, Indiana)

HOOSIER SLIDE. The Hoosier Slide, just west of Michigan City, at 200-feet high, was the largest sand dune on Indiana's lakeshore, and a popular attraction for climbing and sliding. In 20 years, the Ball Brothers of Muncie, Indiana, manufacturers of glass fruit jars, and Pittsburgh Plate Glass of Kokomo, Indiana, carried the Hoosier Slide away in railroad box cars. Northern Indiana Public Service Company (NIPSCO) bought the denuded site to build a power generating plant.

In 1954, Save-the-Dunes Council established an advisory board composed of scientists Edwin Way Teale and Myron Reuben Strong; Bess Sheehan; artist Frank V. Dudley; writers Donald Culross Peattie and Harriet Cowles; conservationist Richard Pough; and philanthropists Mrs. Charles Walgreen and Mrs. Norton W. Barker. With increasing press coverage, the activities of the Council and its advisory board gained wide notoriety and support. (Photos courtesy of Save-the-Dunes Council, Michigan City, Indiana.)

EARL H. REED. Earl H. Reed was the earliest artist of note in the duneland. He did sketching of the landscape over the dunes area from New Buffalo to Miller along the Lake Michigan shores as early as 1891. As a young man he worked as a reporter on the old *Chicago Times*. He was a leader in the campaign which resulted in the establishment of the Dunes State Park by the Indiana legislature. Reed later became a grain broker at the Chicago Board of Trade. As a relief from business Reed would ride the South Shore train from his Chicago home to the dune county where he did his etchings. Reed laid the groundwork for the Save-the-Dunes Council. He testified in Washington before the Mather Committee in 1917. That committee's report was titled "Report on the Proposed Sand Dunes National Park-Indiana." (Photos courtesy of Save-The-Dunes Council, Michigan City, Indiana.)

POLITICAL SUPPORT TO SAVE THE DUNES. Pictured in the top photograph, left to right, are Mrs. Buell, Representative Madden, Mayor Chacharis, Mayor Daley, Mayor Jeorse, Senator Douglas, Mayor Berik, Senator Bible, Mayor Dowling, and Secretary of the Interior Stewart Udall.

Save-the-Dunes Council repeatedly solicited the Indiana Congressional Delegation to introduce legislation preserving the lakeshore by incorporating the dunes into the National Park System. A resounding "no" came from the industry-minded solons. It was in this context that the Save-the-Dunes Council looked outside Indiana for a champion of the dunes, namely Paul H. Douglas, U.S. Senator from neighboring Illinois. Although from Illinois, Douglas was no stranger to the Indiana Dunes. Following his 1931 marriage to Emily Taft, daughter of sculptor Lorado Taft, the couple build a summer cottage in the dunes.

Dorothy Buell first approached Douglas to sponsor a bill to authorize an "Indiana Dunes National Park" in the spring of 1957. Fittingly, he unveiled the bill to establish "Indiana Dunes National Monument" in Dorothy Buell's home on Easter Sunday, 1958. He cited the popularity of the Save-the-Dunes Council as an indication of widespread public support enabling him to go against the wishes of Indiana's political and business community.

Nevertheless, Paul Douglas introduced his bill, S. 3898, on May 26, 1958. It provided for an Indiana Dunes National Monument composed of 3,800 acres in the Central Dunes. (Photos courtesy of Save-the-Dunes Council, Michigan City, Indiana.)

MIDWEST STEEL SITE BEFORE PLANT ERECTION. Senator Douglas introduced the first of many bills in the U.S. Senate to preserve the Indiana Dunes. A 1963 "compromise" between Port promoters and Dunes supporters was worked out at the federal level: most of the unspoiled area between Ogden Dunes and Dune Acres would go to port (and steel mill) development; and a 10,000-acre National Park would be created.

Senator Douglas is cited for his continuing efforts in the U.S. Senate to save some of the natural shoreline of significant sand dunes along Lake Michigan. He was the original advocate of legislation to preserve the Indiana Dunes and, along with dedicated citizen-support from Dorothy Buell, fought an eight-year battle. (Photos courtesy of Save-the-Dunes Council, Michigan City, Indiana.)

PORT OF INDIANA SITE BEFORE INSTALLATION. (Photos courtesy of Save-the-Dunes Council, Michigan City, Indiana.)

**SLIP FOR BARGES HAULING SAND TO NORTHWESTERN UNIVERSITY, EVANSTON, ILLINOIS'
OFF-CAMPUS SITE, AT THE PORT SITE, 1964.** While still at the University of Chicago,
Douglas pioneered in developing plans for a federal old-age pension plan (later called Social
Security), unemployment compensation, and theories stressing the relationship of adequate
wages to high productivity. Although he later found himself at odds with steel mill *owners* over
their plans for plant expansion at the Dunes, factory *workers* were always among his biggest
supporters.

Douglas married twice, first to Dorothy Wolff, a sociologist, and later to Emily Taft, daughter
of the sculptor Lorado Taft. Emily Douglas was herself a U.S. Congressional representative from
1944 to 1946, and she later worked tirelessly alongside her husband in the decade-long effort
to create a national park at the Dunes. Douglas had four children by his first marriage, one by
his second. (Photos courtesy of Save-The-Dunes Council, Michigan City, Indiana.)

AIR VIEW LOOKING OVER BURNS DITCH, 1964, MIDWEST STEEL SITE. (Photos courtesy of
Save-the-Dunes Council, Michigan City, Indiana.)

WESTCHESTER TOWNSHIP LINE ROAD—HEART OF BETHLEHEM PROPERTY, 1960. Douglas took a leave of absence from the University in 1939 when he was elected to represent his Hyde Park neighborhood on the Chicago city council. When the country went to war in 1941, he decided to run for the U.S. Senate as an independent but was defeated.

Looking for an alternate way to serve his country, the 50-year-old former pacifist then enlisted in the Marine Corps as a private. It was said he pulled political strings for the only time in his career to get waivers for age and poor eyesight.

Fighting in the Pacific, he won two Purple Hearts for wounds and a Bronze Star for transporting ammunition under fire. The second wound, suffered in Okinawa, permanently crippled his left arm and ended his military career. He was discharged as a lieutenant colonel in 1946. He was offered a disability pension but never used it; he claimed it never kept him from holding a job.

When in 1948 he ran again for the Senate, this time with Democratic Party backing, he won by 407,000 votes. (Photos courtesy of Save-the-Dunes Council, Michigan City, Indiana)

HIGH POINT WHERE BENCH MARK STOOD. DOUGLAS CLIMBED IT. (Photos courtesy of Save-The-Dunes Council, Michigan City, Indiana.)

CBS-TV INTERVIEW WITH DOUGLAS IN HOME OF DOROTHY BUELL, 1963. Paul Douglas, along with other backers of the park, remained courteous but determined. "I'm not against industrial expansion," he argued; he just objected to the proposed sites for growth "on dunes of incomparable and irreplaceable beauty." As the negotiations wore on, parcels of dune and marsh and forest were committed to industrial development while none were approved for preservation. The park that Congress eventually authorized was a tribute to Douglas' bargaining skill. It contained more than twice the amount of land he had requested in his first bill. The Act that established the Lakeshore on November 5, 1966, encompassed 8,330 acres. Subsequent expansion enlarged the boundaries to 13,023 acres.

Struggle was not new to Paul Douglas when he began his fight to save the Dunes. "When I was young I wanted to save the world," he once commented wryly. "In my middle years I have been content to save my country. Now I just want to save the Dunes." (Photos courtesy of Save-The-Dunes Council, Michigan City, Indiana.)

UDALL, DOUGLAS, AND BIBLE. (Photos courtesy of Save-the-Dunes Council, Michigan City, Indiana.)

SAVE-THE-DUNES BROCHURES. The Save-the-Dunes Council devoted intense scrutiny to the three populated "islands" within the National Lakeshore's boundaries: Dune Acres/Porter Beach, Ogden Dunes, and Beverly Shores. It decided to endorse inclusion of the "Beverly Shores Island," 640 acres, over the other two for a number of reasons. Primarily because Beverly Shores had a lower population density per acre and had clearly outstanding natural values, the Council believed its inclusion could be justified before Congress more easily. Population density differed from town to town. Because three-quarters of the developed portion of Dune Acres was in its northeast quadrant, the "empty" three segments were targeted for inclusion. On the other hand, Beverly Shores' population was scattered throughout its limits and no significant area could be acquired without claiming private homes. The boundaries of the Island were drawn in 1963 by a member of the House Interior Committee concerned with cost-cutting. (Photos courtesy of Save-The-Dunes Council, Michigan City, Indiana.)

SUMMARY

Beverly Shores' planning and architectural history illustrate several major social movements of the past seven decades and how they shaped the built environment. The plan of Beverly Shores and the development image created by its buildings are a significant example of the design affinity for Mediterranean Revival resort suburbs which spread outward from Florida in the 1920s. The town was shaped by a private developer to create an image attractive to the residents of South Chicago who were generally aware of the prestigious resorts in South Florida. When the Depression virtually halted development within the original plan, its developers responded by drawing on the popularity of the Century of Progress World's Fair through the relocation of several of its structures to the resort. The World's Fair buildings are unique remnants of the Fair in themselves, and gain added interest from their role in Beverly Shores. After the rather exclusive resort years of the 1930s, Beverly Shores reflected the thriving industrial development of the 1950s by becoming a balanced community of permanent and seasonal residents. Finally, the impact of the Federal acquisition of two-thirds of the town to create the Indiana Dunes National Lakeshore graphically illustrates the growing sentiment against unchecked development of natural lands which grew in the 1960s and 1970s. The Town of Beverly Shores exists today as a tangible physical product of each of these succeeding currents in American planning, and architectural and social history.